HAGATHA
KITTRIDGE
MUST
DIE

HAGATHA KITTRIDGE MUST DIE

Shelton Keys Dunning

OLDEWOLFF PRINTS

Ramona, California

Oldewolff Prints, a subsidiary of Oldewolff Enterprises
326 Oak St
Ramona, CA 92065
www.oldewolffenterprises.com

Publisher's Note: This is a work of fiction. Names, characters, places, and incidents are a product of the author's imagination. Locales and public names are sometimes used for atmospheric purposes. All trademarks are owned by their respective companies and are denoted by the use of proper capitalization of the company and/or brand. Any resemblance to actual people, living or dead, or to businesses, companies, events, institutions, or locales is completely coincidental.

Book Layout ©2013 BookDesignTemplates.com
Cover Design ©2013 HumbleNations.com

Ordering Information:
Quantity sales. Special discounts are available on quantity purchases by corporations, associations, and others. For details, contact the "Special Sales Department" at the address above.

Hagatha Kittridge Must Die/ Shelton Keys Dunning. – 1st ed.
ISBN 978-1-941319-00-0

To All My Relations

*Please, please remember this story and
these characters are fictitious*

I promise, none of you are reflected in here.

No. Really. Scout's honor.

'Well, son, it is very true nothing in this life is free.
However, there are three things that money cannot buy:
True Love, the Loyalty of a Cat,
and, the most magical of all,
Homegrown Tomatoes."

COLUMBUS ALBAN KITTRIDGE

CHAPTER ONE

Tuesday, 10:00 a.m.

HIS GRANDFATHER'S WAKE wasn't due to start for another two hours, but his mother insisted that he arrive early. Adam Bingham never arrived early for anything. No matter how hard he tried or planned, something always happened and he was perpetually fifteen minutes late.

It made him nervous that he actually made it at ten o'clock on the nose. He checked his watch for the third time, silently pleading with the universe that it was a mere coincidence and not a sign that something wicked was coming. Something besides his great-aunt Agatha – Hagatha behind her back – who was as evil a woman as ever God invented. Agatha simply refused to die.

"Addy, be a dear..." a shrill, dictatorial voice sent banshees looking for someplace to hide.

Adam cringed. He didn't even get a chance to reach the walkway before Hagatha cornered him. He turned to see her silver Cadillac moored in the carport, driver's door ajar, and her largeness attempting to dislodge herself from behind the steering wheel. "Uh," he glanced around searching for some sort of rescue, "Aunt Agatha, my name is Adam, remember?"

Her eyes shriveled him. Without a protective lead suit, he was certain to be sterile now. As the car complained, she fought an arm free. "Insolent boy. Your mother, God help her, didn't have the sense to raise a polite child, did she? Don't just stand there catching flies, help me."

Before his high school graduation, Adam grew six inches in one week. After his first week as a college freshman, he grew another six inches. He towered over a majority of his family at six feet five inches and still Agatha could belittle him until he felt less than an inch tall. She had that effect on everyone. He shuffled towards her Caddy, forsaken. "What do you need help with?"

A stubby leg broke the front seat barrier and stretched out to hover over the cement with her flailing arm. She was halfway out and breathing like a steam engine. "What's it look like?"

It looks like a whale wrestling a rhino. Adam braced his back and offered his arm. "Oh, sure thing."

"Not me, you idiot boy! I'm not a useless cripple. Get the tuna casserole from the trunk."

He was never so grateful to be so insulted. Taking the keys from her flailing hand, he unlocked the trunk and gawked at the size of the casserole. *How in the he...how am I supposed to...how the heck did she get this in here anyway?* It was easily four feet long and two feet deep. He removed his sport coat, set it on the edge of the car, and rolled up his shirt sleeves. He wedged his arms underneath the tuna barge and pulled it from the trunk in one seamless move. Proud, he turned with a smile.

"About time, you lazy cur," she hissed and slammed the trunk closed.

He blinked. The trunk had closed on his coat. The trunk had au-
tomatically locked itself. The keys to the trunk were in the pocket of
his coat. The pocket of his coat was inside the locked trunk. He
blinked again, feeling owlish. "Aunt Agatha," he began.

"Oh speak up Boy, mumbling is rude. I don't know why your
mother, God help her, puts up with you. In some cultures, animals
eat their young." Her excessively rotund arms were folded atop her
behemoth chest, hands tucked into her armpits. Her purple muumuu
stretched around her, failing to bring any hint of ladylike petite-ness
to the mountain majesty. She just stood before him, a giant raisin
mascot, only angrier.

"The keys to your car."

"What of them? Spit it out."

"The keys to your car are now in your trunk."

She pursed her artificially pink lips, a fluid sucking sound sliding
from her teeth. Her breath reeked of denture cleaner. "Well then, I
guess you had better figure out how to get them out, yes?"

He watched the raisin shimmy up the walkway, unable to pull his
attention elsewhere. The wood planks of the porch steps bowed
under her oppressive feet. Getting out of the car seemed a breeze
compared to her attempt to enter the house through the front door.
Adam trudged towards the kitchen door at the back of the house,
demoralized and eager for a shot of whiskey.

With any luck, Cousin Tess had already located the key to the
liquor cabinet.

Adam balanced with the casserole as he managed the knob. He
pushed the back door with his foot and it squealed open on rust-
spotted hinges. Most of the hinges in the old Victorian needed tending to on the first floor. It had been a few months since he helped his

grandfather grease the hardware on the upper floors. Grandpa Lum got sick before Adam could finish the chore.

The kitchen reflected the worn, crooked man that had used it daily since his birth. Adam found space for the tuna barge on the counter-top and shook life back into his arms as he looked about. There was something about his grandfather's passing that seemed to brighten the sagging room. Like a widow free of slaving over a hot stove, the kitchen cast off its miserly existence and basked in the warmth of the sunlight streaming through the windows.

"Adam?"

"In the kitchen, Ma!"

His heart broke when she entered. Her face was pink and puffy, swollen from lack of sleep. "Agatha said you were here. I didn't see your truck."

"I parked down by the bat-cave to leave room for handicappers," he said, referencing the ramshackle barn at the base of the hill.

"Did bats really take the barn over?"

He nodded, "The guano is at least a foot thick in there."

She had the lost look she got when she didn't quite understand the humor of a joke. "It nearly killed him when he had to get rid of his horses. I guess Mother Nature has a way of moving on even when you don't..."

It occurred to him that his mother was now an orphan. He had nothing to say to that could make it any better, so he stood dumb, a cigar-store Indian on the verge of splinters.

"Jesus, Mary and Joseph, what in tarnation's that?" her long finger pointed to the barge.

"Tuna casserole, supposedly."

A laugh escaped before her hands caught her mouth. Her glassy eyes were wide with disbelief. "Not Agatha's?"

"'Fraid so."

"God Almighty. We'll have to slop it to the hogs," she breathed through her fingers.

"Addy! Do you have my keys yet Boy?" Agatha's resonating shriek could just as easily been right at his ear as loud as it was. Before the end of the day, Adam knew his eardrums would be ruptured and his balls rendered ineffectual.

His mother leaned forward after a furtive glance over her shoulder. "What's she going on about? She said you threw her keys in the trunk to be spiteful."

Flash anger struck his voice, "That ungrateful, miserable cow! She's the one who shut the bloody trunk! I put the keys in my pocket before I took off my jacket so I could wrestle that tuna thing from her trunk at her insistence–"

"All right, all right, chill it Adam. Try to keep in mind she just lost a brother. She's bound to be short-tempered."

"Yeah, well, you lost your father, and I lost a grandfather, and death is no excuse for..." he looked up as a shadow crossed the kitchen table. Her purple mountain majesty filled the doorway. "Sorry, H–er–Aunt Agatha. I was just talking to Mom."

"Keys, Addy," she prodded.

"I'll get right on that." He bolted through the back-door before he received another tongue lashing. Breaking into the sunlight like a man free from prison, he sucked in each breath of air. His heart skipped rope with his stomach. Adam wondered if whiskey would be strong enough.

He wondered if he would be strong enough.

He wondered if a jury would convict him of first degree murder if they knew what an unmitigated bitch Hagatha was.

Adam stumbled to the Caddy, allowing every cuss word in every language he ever learned to slip through his teeth. The trunk taunted him. He didn't know one thing about breaking into cars. *Perhaps a crowbar from the tool shed?* He could easily kill a few hours looking for a crowbar in Grandpa's tool shed. A true product of the Great Depression, the man had saved everything from the plastic bindings on Sunday papers to scraps of barbed wire. Since his tetanus shot was current, all Adam had to worry about was the occasional black widow. *Easy Peasy.*

He nodded once to himself, setting his resolve, and walked back up the carport to the garden path at the back of the house. Now overgrown and in desperate need of some TLC, the garden had gone to seed and weed. A breeze stirred the tired tomato vine near the pavers, filling the air with the pungent, earthy scent. His grandfather said once that of all the plants that graced his garden, tomatoes were the stubborn buggers that gave him as much pain as they gave him joy, and every single one of them had come up volunteer. A tear arrived with a smile and Adam paused for a moment just to greet the coming memories.

Honesty parted his lips. "I'm gonna miss you, Grandpa Lum."

From the depths of the weeds behind him, a low hiss-like growl drifted into the garden. Adam turned to find Sauerkraut, the yellow feral barn cat, glaring back. Her eyes were fully dilated and her tongue hung out cigarette-like from the side of her mouth. Sauerkraut hissed again, rolled over and rubbed her face against some heart-shaped green leaves.

"Ah, caught you in the catnip did I?" Adam chuckled. She appeared to be more concerned with her fix than with him, but he gave her a wide berth anyway. Sauerkraut was an efficient mouser and a ruthless devil towards anyone who wasn't Grandpa Lum. Adam pitied her. With his grandfather's passing, she would more than likely be put down. *Maybe she would go unnoticed?* He cast a warning over his shoulder, "Hey, keep out of sight, eh? Just in case?"

The cat made a noise that sounded more like a pigeon's coo, squeezed her eyes, and drooled.

CHAPTER TWO

Tuesday, 10:30 a.m.

T HE TOOL SHED WAS MUSTY. It showed signs of being orga-
nized once upon a time, but like the garden, objects were
discarded and forgotten. Dust was captured in cobwebs, spider webs,
and in layers so thick it supported its own ecosystem. Adam's eyes
still weren't adjusted to the meager light that trickled through the
crud-covered window. He was molested by a garden rake and
tripped up by empty paint cans before he found the light switch. The
fluorescent shop light snapped and hissed to life, chasing shadows to
their recesses. The light helped but hung around the room with an
impatient glow.

"Crowbar, crowbar," he sang to the collective buckets of nails
and screws as he moved them to access the spaces behind them. "O
the driving crowbar."

"You're singing that wrong. It's the driving snow."

Adam spun around, nearly tripping over a gas canister, to see
who belonged to the other voice in the shed. The owner was a twen-
ty-something woman with frazzled strawberry blonde hair cascading
from underneath a knit cap, clutching a patchwork teddy bear tight
to her chest. She leaned against the doorframe, wide eyes soaking in

the room. "Uh, right. But," he said approaching her, dusting his hand off before offering it, "I'm actually looking for a crowbar."

She clutched the teddy bear tighter and backed up, "Sorry, I don't...People and I, well we..."

He absorbed her terrified look for a moment as his hands tucked into the pockets of his slacks. "I'm Adam. Adam Bingham. Lum was my grandfather."

She stopped her retreat and nodded, neglecting to make eye contact. "He showed me your picture once. You're the tall one. My name is December Ashby. I was born in April though. My parents named me that because they hate me. Mr. Kittridge is my, was my neighbor."

"What makes you think your parents hate you?"

A vacant look descended upon her countenance. She fidgeted with the worn ears of her bear. "They left me at a vegetable stand just outside of Sacramento with a twenty dollar bill safety-pinned to my sweater."

"Oh." He just trespassed where he didn't really want to go. She was way too calm for his liking. He grappled his small-talk-arsenal for a quick change of topic and latched on to her stuffed animal. "Uh, what's your bear's name?"

"Snoopy."

"You named a bear Snoopy?"

Her previously vacant face flashed him a sharp look, "No, the bear's name is Teddy. You're being snoopy."

A sigh gurgled in his throat. First Hagatha, then Sauerkraut, and now a complete stranger seemed to support the universal plot against him. He turned back to his crowbar hunt without another word and tried to ignore December's lingering presence in the doorway. *Tess will be here soon, and it'll be beer o'clock somewhere.* Adam fumbled through his grandfather's hoard, passing over scraps of tin and copper, and several tackle boxes filled with melted jiggers.

"What do you need it for?"

He rocked up to his feet and pivoted, ducking again at the next cabinet. "What?"

"The crowbar, what do you need it for?"

"Snoopy." The word was out before he could censor his mouth. He didn't want to be as rude as it sounded. He peered over his shoulder to catch her reaction, bracing himself for the flood of apologies tripping around his teeth.

To his surprise and great relief, she giggled. "That's so very fair. I mean, I'm not good with people. I never have been. Auntie Jean said I even peed on the doctors at birth."

Too much information. He coughed to cover his wince only to feel a smile tugging at his mouth. "My aunt Agatha locked her keys in the trunk. I thought I could pop it open with a crowbar."

"Sure if you want to fuck up the locking mechanism." Swearing didn't seem to bother her. "Why don't you use the trunk release latch?"

"It hasn't worked since 1992."

"You could just get the spare set of keys from the house."

"Which house?" Disbelief asked. "Grandpa's house?"

She frowned, "Duh. Mr. Kittridge got the spare set eons ago, like back when his stinkin' sister still had her own teeth. Mr. Kittridge was tired of his stinkin' sister lying about locking her keys in the car when it was time for her to leave. He'd sometimes leave the spare set on the back porch for me and I'd joyride it down to the Five'n'Dime, just to mess with his stinkin' sister's head. He'd laugh and laugh afterwards and she'd just turn all red and spit when she spoke."

"I'd've paid good money to see that." He rose, knocking an oil-can off of its perch. "Craptastic," he stared in dismay at the splatter across his upper thigh. "That's not going to look right. The both of us leaving the shed and me with a crotch stain."

"Why would that not look right?" she asked. Her face was glowing with a soft innocence.

He bit his tongue, embarrassed that his mind went to the gutter and he had used his out-loud voice. "Never mind."

"Oh, no wait, I get it. It's like I was in here and we were–"

"Yes, exactly," he cut her off, feeling a blush forming.

"Well, what do you want to do then?"

I want to get Hagatha off of my back. "Let's go find the keys to the Caddy. It's a family affair, so no one should be looking at my crotch anyway."

They shut the shed up and walked in silence towards the house, December a few paces behind Adam. She made him nervous. The way she held on to her bear wasn't normal for someone in her age bracket, and the comment about being abandoned near Sacramento didn't help him feel any safer. Crazy was a weakness for him, as his last girlfriend proved. He filed a restraining order in the end of that relationship.

Sauerkraut was gone when they passed through the garden, the vegetation pressed into the earth where she had been. Not knowing where she was, however, played to his fears of being randomly attacked. The cat was a super ninja. He swallowed hard and quickened his pace, nearly knocking Tess over as he rounded the corner. "Crap, sorry Tess. You okay?"

"Yeah, I was just looking for you," she pushed a flask in his hand. "Hagatha's already dug into my craw. There is no way we're getting through this day sober."

He unscrewed the stopper and sniffed the contents before knocking back a shot. He coughed as Kentucky bourbon burned out his insides. "Do you," he paused to breathe, "know December?"

Her nod was stiff, "Hi December."`

"Tess, I've less to confess, but sure I jest when I rest for sleep does not last." December babbled, her eyes bright as stars.

"Still the same wackadoo I see," she accused.

"I'm not wackadoo," December's words were firm. "I'm just big-souled."

"You're wackadoo," Tess reiterated. "Shot?"

December put the bear's nose to her ear, as if to listen to its secret. After an awkward moment passed, she shook her head negative. Adam gave another cough, uncomfortable with the silence. "Sooo Tess, I need to grab Grandpa's spare keys to Hagatha's Caddy. Do you know where he kept them?"

Her left eyebrow tucked tightly against her nose. "What makes you think I know where he kept anything?"

"Please. You know where they buried Jimmy Hoffa."

She snorted and took a swig from the flask. "They didn't bury him. They chopped him up into chum and airdropped him over the Everglades. Anyway, I've already scoured the back porch and the mudroom in search of the liquor cabinet key. No spares. No keys of any kind."

Adam groaned and swiped the flask back, taking a long drink in the process. "Well, my suggestion is we continue your search for the liquor key. Maybe we'll luck out and find Hagatha's spare key then."

"Hey what's wrong with your pants?" Tess pointed to his upper thigh.

"I had a disagreement with an oil-can. Why, does it look bad?"

"It doesn't look good."

He shrugged. "Well, if I get desperate, I'll raid Grandpa's closet."

When the trio reached the back porch, December broke away to investigate the heather under the railing. Adam paused, ascertaining if her attention wandered. She jumped up, however, and followed them in the kitchen. "He didn't leave the keys for me this time." Her voice crossed from another world, ethereal and feathery. The bear she brought to her shoulder as if to burp it.

Just beneath the bear's stubby tail where a small safety-pin kept a hole from unraveling, the words Póg mo thóin were stitched into the patchwork fur. Adam was tempted to ask about it when Agatha appeared. "Addy, you really can't keep a single thought in that pea-brain of yours, can you? Are you one of those pot-head derelicts?"

Before Adam could respond, Tess dragged him from the room. "He's working on it, Agatha."

"And do please remember if it doesn't strain your feeble mind to greet your family. Uncle Curd and Aunt Dahlia are in the living room." Agatha called after them as she opened the refrigerator door. Adam turned in time to catch December twisting her middle finger at the old woman's back. He liked her in that moment, without reservation.

The living room was rearranged to accommodate extra chairs, mostly the never-used beach chairs that Grandpa stored in the cellar. Uncle Curtis occupied the worn recliner tucked into the corner of the room, where his snores echoed against the yellowed walls. Nearby, Adam's mother conversed with her sister Dahlia, both crying.

Tess didn't bother to stop as she pulled Adam through to the cellar staircase. "Dad's been up all night and Mom's not handling anything well. I'll bet Agatha just wanted you to interrupt everyone." Tess breathed through her teeth. "That woman would do us all a favor if she'd just take a hint and drop dead."

The cellar door screeched open, suffering from the same rusty-hinge-disease as the back door. Fascinated, Adam watched while December set Teddy on the steps and hocked phlegm from her throat to spit on the complaining hinges. "What?" she barked. "Why are you looking at me?"

Tess reiterated her sentiment. "Yup, completely wackadoo."

CHAPTER THREE

Tuesday, 11:15 a.m.

THE CELLAR WAS DESIGNED for fruit and veg storage and as such, was free of damp. Adam chuckled softly, remembering the jack-o-lanterns he begged his grandfather to save. Every Christmas, Adam would rush down to the cellar to check on the carved pumpkins. He didn't realize until he was much older that his grandfather carved new ones each Thanksgiving to replace the previous decayed pumpkins.

As a flood of random memories washed through him, December danced about the empty spaces over the concrete floor as if no one watched her. Adam did his best to stay out of her way, side-stepping her when his attempts failed. Tess investigated the apothecary drawers of the wall cabinet at a speed Adam thought impractical. She was twice as likely to overlook the keys even if they stared her in the face.

The twins stumbled down the steps then. Chase and Chance dressed like matching hoodlums, their tent-sized jeans barely defying gravity, gripping Christmas red boxers just below their hips. Adam frowned. Were Tess and he the only grandkids who bothered to dress for the occasion?

"Your Ma said you was down here," Chance announced, leering molester-like at December. "Hey there sweet-cheeks, it's so good to be dreaming again."

Adam bristled, "Smooth, Genius. Real smooth."

"That's me, smooth as a Ferrari 458 Spider and just as hot," Chance gloated, inching closer to the strawberry-blonde with a slithery gait and his hand on his crotch like a gangster wannabe.

December snatched her bear from his perch and ducked beneath the staircase. "Ugh, spiders."

Adam laughed at his cousin's confused look. "Well I don't think she's impressed."

Chance squared his shoulders, "Oh that so? What, you got a market on the girl? Am I about to steal your girl out from underneath your nose?"

"Sure, think what you want." Adam turned to help Tess blaze through the drawers. "Can't fix stupid."

"What'chya-lookin-fo?" Chase mumbled. Grandpa Lum called him Mashed-Potato-Mouth. Chase's words always mushed together so they were indistinguishable from each other. Strangers never understood a word he said.

"Hagatha locked her keys in the trunk and blamed it on Adam," Tess piped up. There was irritation in her voice. Adam wondered if she was sore at the twins, at December, or at the lack of a liquor cabinet key. She continued her explanation. "There's a spare set of keys for the Caddy floating about, and we think the liquor key is with them."

"I hate spiders. They have three too many legs." December whined from her hiding spot. "Or is it centipedes that have three too many?"

Tess slammed her last drawer into its socket. "God, December, can you forget you're a wackadoo for a few seconds and help us? The sooner we get Hagatha off of Adam's back, the sooner we'll be able to drink ourselves blind and give Grandpa Lum a proper send off."

"I told you, I'm not wackadoo. I'm big-souled!" the bear-hugger screeched.

"What are you even doing here anyway?" Tess stomped around the stairs, shoving Chase out of her way. "What was Grandpa to you?"

Tears welled up in her eyes as she replied, "He was the only one who ever told me stories about family and love in all their stupid glory. He was the only one who never called me vile names. He made me feel safe and wanted, like if my world went to shit, it'd be okay 'cause Mr. Kittridge would send in the Marines. He treated me like I *mattered*. And now that he's gone, I'm back to being the girl no parents wanted with a family that doesn't give a shit."

The cousins exchanged glances in the silence that followed. December sniffed and wiped her eyes. Huddled beneath the staircase like a forgotten ragdoll, she clung tight to her ever-constant bear and wept. Adam wanted to do something but felt trapped. Emotional women paralyzed him. All he could do, to his shame, was stand and watch her face leak.

"Look-pot-bears!" Chase pointed to a shadowed corner where a giant collection of plastic bear-shaped cookie jars were piled.

Chance was the first to move, followed close by his twin and then Tess. Adam, however, was still locked in position, unable to stop December's tears. "I didn't know," he whispered, willing himself to crouch low, to be at eye level with her. "I didn't know," he repeated, unable to find any other words.

She looked at him with big glassy eyes and a soggy grin, "I know you didn't know, but I know you. You're the tall one who would fetch his cane and his pills and rake his lawn without ever being asked. You fixed his glasses and unblocked his toilet and made it so he could still watch his television when everything went digital."

A knot developed in his throat so fast, Adam nearly choked. All these things he did, and yet he didn't remember. And he would never be able to do them for Grandpa Lum again. Pain seared his heart and he was paralyzed once more.

"You were the tall one and you listened to every story he ever told. You mucked out the stables when he still had horses and collected eggs when he still had chickens. And the wood! You were the tall one who could chop two cords of wood for the fireplace without tiring. Mr. Kittridge said you'd walk through spider-webs so he didn't have to." December raised a hand as if to touch his face, but returned it quickly to her bear. She stroked the patchwork as if to comfort him. After a long moment, she whispered, "Mr. Kittridge didn't like spiders either."

"Adam, did you hear? Grandpa's a pothead!" Tess squealed at him from across the room.

The words made no sense. Adam stood up, puzzled, late to the punch-line. Tess displayed a bear container much like Teddy had been first displayed, dried sprigs of weeds visible within the clear plastic. The containers once held animal crackers, but like so many other things in Grandpa's possession, they found a new purpose. And according to Tess, that purpose was to store marijuana. The twins looked just as confused, but there was hunger behind their eyes. In a perverse world, they had hit a jackpot.

December launched from her shelter, discarding her bear, and ripped the canister from Tess's hands. "That's not pot."

"What is it then? He's got a million of these plastic bears stacked over here filled with this crap."

Chance unscrewed the lid of one and sniffed overzealous at the released air. "I dunno, but she's right. It ain't pot."

Tess rubbed her forehead. "I thought Grandpa was a hoarder, but what could he possibly have wanted with all this...whatever it is?"

Adam spied a familiar heart-shaped leaf through the plastic and breathed with relief. Everything was right with the world again. "It's catnip."

Chance made a face, "Catnip?"

"For Sauerkraut," December stated, a confident smile stretched across her pink-streaked face.

"I didn't know you made sauerkraut out of catnip."

"Not the food, Genius," Adam barked, irked that Chance didn't know anything about Grandpa's life. "Sauerkraut's the barn mouser."

"Oh," he nodded dumbly and inhaled the air again.

"Christ, you're going to try and smoke it anyway, aren't you?" Tess spat and turned on her heels. "Come on Adam. We still need to find those keys."

Chase tapped her on the shoulder. "Why-don't-we-just-pick-the-lock?"

"Pick the lock?" Tess repeated, her brow furrowed.

He nodded, "I-can-do-it."

"You?" Adam hoped against hope.

"It'll-cost-you-though."

Tess crossed her arms and glared, her ears turning red. "Cost us? I don't think so, Chase. You'll do it or I'll tell your mother that you stole money from her live-it-up-fund to pay for Amanda Keaton's abortion after your idiot brother knocked her up."

Chase turned three shades of invisible, "Okie-dokie-I'll-do-it-fo-nothin'."

"Get your ass up there," Tess snapped. She wheeled about to his twin, "And you, stop huffing the catnip and move!"

Chance dropped the jar and tried to smuggle a handful of the herb into his jean pocket. Tess ripped it from his hands and pushed him forward before she handed the weed off to Adam. December fell in line behind the others already moving up the stairs. Without thinking, Adam shoved the catnip in his pocket and trailed after his cousins.

Grandpa's armchair still housed the snoring Uncle Curtis, despite Agatha's shrill cackling from the other side of the room. Extended family and friends dressed in somber blacks and grays milled about with drinks in hand. Some wrought handkerchiefs between their fingers while others conversed in hushed voices. Adam struggled to match faces with names, but his mind felt disconnected. The scene was growing more dismal by the moment. After Chase broke into the trunk, they would have to make him break into the liquor cabinet. Tess was right. There was no way to get through this mess with any measure of sobriety.

December delighted Adam once again by flipping another bird at Hagatha's back.

The gang sneaked by the mourners as quick as they could, engaging the gathered only when spoken to. Adam's mother caught him by the arm as he attempted to exit the front door. "What happened to your slacks?"

Adam almost forgot the oil-can incident. He opened his mouth to reply when he heard Hagatha cackle again. The words "I'll explain later" tumbled out before his teeth could check them. "How are you holding up?"

Her bottom lip quivered. Her voice dropped to barely above a whisper. "I think I'd be fine if Aunt Agatha wasn't making everyone such a nervous wreck. The preacher's convinced she's a demon sent from hell. You know Rev McCleary. He doesn't speak ill of anyone."

"She's horrible, but I think everyone loved Grandpa so much that they'll deal with her."

"Cousin Candy said we should have her put down like a rabid dog." Tears developed in her already puffy eyes.

"Look, Mom, I know you only want to keep the peace, but Agatha breeds chaos wherever she goes. You're only going to end up making yourself sick over her. It's not worth it."

She squeezed his chin, "Thank you for being here. Your father...just thank you."

He gave her the best chin-up smile he could muster and walked out the front door.

CHAPTER FOUR

Tuesday, 12:00 p.m.

C HASE KNELT AT THE TRUNK, manipulating a piece of wire in the Caddy's lock. "I'll-get-her-done-in-five."

Tess shook her head and took out her cell phone. "I'm gonna call triple A. I get the distinct impression this ain't gonna work."

Adam glanced about. "Where's December?"

"Not my turn to babysit," she hissed.

"Nice, Tess. Can't you tell the girl–"

"The girl what?" she interrupted. "I'm supposed to feel sorry for her and treat her with kid gloves simply because she's broken? I'm not related to her, so I don't have to put up with her sh - Hi yes my name is Tess Archer...yes I'll hold." She took a deep breath. "Shit if I don't want to."

"Yeah but –"

"Don't you 'yeah but' me Adam. You've got a thing for crazy and I don't think you're thinking with the correct brain. And since you're my favorite cousin, I'm obligated to tell you she's a whole steaming pile of damage."

"Crap-this-isn't-working," Chase looked up from the trunk. "If-I-can't-get-it-open, you-still-gonna-tell-ma?"

Tess ran a frustrated hand through her hair. "No, Chase, I'm not gonna tell your mother. Look, we'll get triple – Hi yes, I just locked my keys in the trunk. Is there any way you can get a locksmith out to Pine Valley at Eagle Canyon?"

Adam risked another glance around and caught Chance nursing his jaw at the end of the driveway. He left the car to Tess and hailed the other hoodlum brother with a brisk jog. "Chance, have you seen December?"

"She punched me then ran off across the field." He waved a hand to the neighbor's bull pasture.

"Damn it Chance! What did you do?"

He looked truly appalled. "What did I do? I didn't do nothing. All I did was invite her to the party in my pants."

"Really?" Adam shook his head in disbelief. "I don't know what's more pathetic. The fact that you thought that line would work or that you're shocked she punched you. Geez."

"Yeah, well I thought you said she wasn't yours! Why do you care?" Adam heard as he trotted back up the drive. December's cellar confession had sparked something within him. He wanted to speak to her about Grandpa again, about how all their crazy lives intertwined. Her running now meant he lost a connection he wasn't willing to give up just yet. December was such a hair-trigger, he wondered if she'd ever come back.

Tess and Chase met him halfway. "The auto club said an hour, maybe two." Tess announced, her mouth drawn in a thin line. "Do you think we can tolerate Hagatha's abuse that long?"

Adam shrugged. He felt tired and a little lost. He remembered his mother's remark about the effect Hagatha was having on everybody and straightened his back. "Well, since we don't have much of a choice, I guess I can take it if it gives her someone to focus her anger on. The more she berates me, the less she berates everyone else."

"Hagatha'll-be-a-bitch-to-everyone-anyway," Chase cast his eyes downward, his feet shuffling in mud-caked Airwalks. "I-wish-someone'd-push-her-off-the-roof."

Tess rolled her eyes and laughed. The anger was gone from her tone. "She wouldn't fit up that nineteenth century staircase."

"So do we have a backup plan to get into the liquor cabinet?" Blank looks answered his question. A tired ache licked at his bones and Adam gave a weary sigh, "Well, it's time for lunch, I'm sure. Let's head to the kitchen and make sure the tuna casserole disposed of properly."

Chance trotted up the path, tugging his pants up over his butt. "I don't see Todd's Porsche anywhere. Do you think he's gonna show?"

Tess frowned, "Uncle Todd's gotta show. He's got the will."

"I doubt he'd bring the Porsche out on this road. He always had the Land Rover when he visited Grandpa." Adam scanned the parked cars, but saw no evidence of Todd's attendance. "Come on, I'm sure he'll show up. I don't know about you all but my stomach thinks my throat's been cut."

The foursome wandered towards the kitchen door. The distinct aromas of a family potluck drifted through the open windows as they passed under. Their fare rarely varied from occasion to occasion. Always present were a couple of fried chicken buckets, courtesy of Cousin Mike. Petal brought the potato salad, Jim the venison roast, and Tanya the champ. Sissy provided mixed green salads and her homemade Vidalia onion dressing. Grandpa Lum would've brought tomatoes.

Adam stopped where the path broke off to the garden and debated salvaging a few tomatoes for the luncheon. Tess noticed his hesitation, "What?"

"Uh, you go on ahead. I'll be there in a second." Adam broke away and returned to the garden.

Tomatoes hid under tangled vines, most green globes of young fruit. He parted leaves in several places, crouching low to the earth, ignoring the soil that crept into his shoes. The fragrant plants made him a little heady in the sun, but Adam was determined to find a few ripe gems. After a few minutes, he settled for five large, mostly orange tomatoes and cradled them carefully in his arms. Pride filled his heart and he imagined his grandfather smiling, happy someone thought to fetch his contribution.

He climbed the back steps, careful of his cargo. A shrill screech erupted from within the kitchen, rooting him to the porch. The distinct grumblings of a pissed-off cat followed and a large purple blur exploded through the whining door. Hagatha's screaming mass knocked him over in her flight and Adam closed his eyes against the knowledge of the pain involved with a head collision.

Someone unleashed the fury of the garden hose at Sauerkraut. He heard the tell-tale whooshing of water and hissing of an angry cat amid stifled giggles and shoo-cats. Adam told himself to get up, but his arms and legs refused to respond. An unfamiliar dampness leached through his shirt and he tried to make sense of it in the dark world behind his eyelids.

He heard his mother scream. "Adam! No, God. Adam!"

His eyes flew open. His mother's face was a pink-streaked mask of fear and panic. "Mom?"

"God, okay. Don't worry. You'll be fine." The gentle pressure of her hand on his chest accompanied her frenzied whisper.

Shit! The tomatoes! "Mom, wait! I'm okay. It's not blood; it's tomatoes." He willed his arms to move, to prop him up from the porch, to show his mother he wasn't at Death's door. "I knocked my head, but I'm fine."

She slapped his shoulder. "Don't ever do that, ever again!"

Adam was sure that his mother would look back on this someday and realize tomato stains look nothing like blood, that the stress of the day made the scene worse than it was. He didn't point out the green crowns plastered to the orangey ooze across his shirt. "I won't Mom, I promise."

Tess appeared in the doorway, her laughter evaporating. "Adam?"

"I'm fine," he reiterated. Once again the spotlight was pointed his direction and he really didn't want to be the star of the show. "What happened in there?"

A broad smile dispelled the worry from his mother's face. "Oh it was classic. The kitchen was packed with everyone trying to get food when Aunt Agatha noticed Sauerkraut standing knee deep in her tuna casserole. I wish we'd caught that on video. We'd've won the grand prize on the funny videos show for sure."

Adam chuckled in spite of himself and looked down at his crushed tomatoes. "Well, it worked in theory."

"Dad would've thanked you for the effort." His mother sighed, wiping fresh tears from her eyes. "And I appreciate the thought. It would've been perfect."

Tess shook her head. "What would've been perfect is Agatha slipping off the top of the stairs and plummeting to her death."

His mother shot her a look. "That's a callous thing to say, Tessie Glynne."

Adam glanced about, searching for the signs of a lingering Hagatha. "Well, the day's still young, Tess, you might yet get your wish."

His mother slugged him.

CHAPTER FIVE

Tuesday, 1:00 p.m.

A DAM PULLED A PAIR OF GRAY SLACKS from a hanger at the back his grandfather's closet. It carried with it the sharp scent of cedar, a fragrance that Adam always found refreshing. The throb in his head dulled for a moment and he was able to find solace in the quiet room. His grandmother's keepsakes were still honored treasures displayed in pictures on the walls and knick-knacks on the nightstands. He felt both at home and as if he were trespassing, a happy tug-of-war of emotions. For all that passed, his grandparents would live forever in his memories. The idea made him smile.

He donned a worn gray and green plaid flannel, also borrowed from the closet, and rolled the sleeves up passed his elbows. His belt cinched the waist in tighter than the slacks were used to. A fresh pair of socks remanded from the chest of drawers finished his appropriated look. Catnip fell from his stained clothes as he bundled them together, and he scooped it up and stuffed it in the new pockets. Leaving catnip on his grandfather's bedroom floor somehow seemed irreverent.

His grandmother's soft eyes smiled at him from her portrait next to the door. He smiled back, gloom lifting from his shoulders. The day was bound to get better.

A soft knock sounded at the door before it opened. Tess handed him a plastic grocery bag, "Todd's here."

"Ah." Adam stuffed his clothes in the bag and followed her out into the creaky hallway. The floor sang a ballad of katydids as they passed, the history of the house oozing silently through the hickory boards. "He'll be disappointed he missed all the excitement."

Tess snorted as they descended the narrow staircase, "Doubtful. Hagatha cornered him and his latest bimbo the moment they walked through the front door. I always knew she was cruel but I never thought she was this greedy."

"Why? What did you overhear?"

"She's asking how quickly she can tear this house apart and put the property up for sale."

"What!" Adam stopped halfway down. "Grandpa Lum wouldn't leave this house to her. He knows she never liked it and can't work the land. What's she playing at?"

Tess shrugged, "That's not all. Apparently she wants the money so she can take – quote – a well-deserved vacation – unquote."

"A vacation from what?"

"Why, from taking care of her invalid brother, of course."

Rage at an epic scale saturated every fiber of his being. "Like Hell she took care of him."

"Welcome to Hagatha's world. You're just renting the space, and you're not paying enough."

"I suddenly don't give a shit if we ever get her car keys out. To Hell with her."

The macabre family reunion stuffed the living room beyond safe occupancy. Adam negotiated his way to the coat closet to dispose of his laundry, and wormed a path through the sea of cousins to his mother. "I've always liked that flannel," she mentioned, straightening his collar. "It suits you."

"Thanks Mom. After the morning I've had, I wanted something comforting." He debated about bringing up Hagatha's greed, but a volcano of fury was simmering under his skin and the last thing he wanted was to create a scene his mother would be ashamed of.

"What's wrong?" His mother's intuition served her well. She studied him with intensity, her lie-detector look boring into his mind.

"Nothing. I'm just pissed at Grandpa Lum's stinkin' sister, is all." He searched the room for his compatriots. Seated with her parents, Tess still wore the look of disgust she had for most of the day. Chase and Chance were nowhere to be seen. Positioned in front of the fireplace, Uncle Todd winked a greeting; a curvaceous blonde cozied up beside him. "I like Todd's new flavor."

His mother elbowed his ribcage, "Stop it Adam."

"C'mon Mom, you gotta admit, the man has taste."

"An acquired taste, yes," she replied, grinning. "Lord, but they do seem to get younger and younger around him. This one apparently is promoting her own line of elegant dog-collars."

"Really? Looks like she's promoting playmate of the month." The comment earned him another ribbing.

Someone coughed in the dining room doorway behind him. December, her ever-vacant stare affixed to her face, stood bear-less at the antique table. "You changed?"

"Uh, yeah, short, embarrassing story. I'll tell you later. Do you know Mom? December, Eileen. Mom, December. She's grandpa's neighbor."

"Oh, Jeanie's...niece right?" His mom offered a hand that went unaccepted.

"Sorry, I don't do the touching thing well," December said, her voice laced with fear.

"Oh, right. Dad mentioned you were guarded. I forgot."

December lit up, her eyes bright and hopeful. "Mr. Kittridge mentioned me?"

"Often, and fondly. He said that you always brought sunshine into his home." Warmth emanated from her response. "For that I thank you."

"Think nothing of it, Mrs. Bingham," December beamed even brighter. "Mr. Kittridge was my favoritest person in the whole world."

"Thank you for being here."

Todd called for everyone's attention. Adam caught Hagatha's smug glare from across the room. She was perched rather precariously upon a dainty Shaker chair, like a bear in a circus act defying laws of nature and physics. He heard the slurping sound of her teeth adjusting and he shivered.

"Well now, I have the unpleasant task of imparting Dad's wishes as executor of his estate." Todd sounded professional and lawyerly. "I insisted I wouldn't take a penny for this position. I could never take the old man's money like he wanted me to. Even after I landed the partnership with Macey, Billings, and Hyde, even after my first year bonus netted half his whole life's earnings, he still wanted to give me an allowance. Columbus Alban Kittridge was an amazing, kindhearted soul, and his presence will be missed."

Adam swallowed the lump in his throat and thought to get a glass of water. His mom, new tears cascading down her face, forced him to abandon the idea and he wrapped his arm around her shoulders. This was the role his father should have had, but his military service kept him absent and regretful. Adam hugged his mother tight for his father's sake.

Todd coughed, soliciting a busty sigh from his companion and another sucking sound from Hagatha. He proceeded with decorum, listing assets with numbers and associated names that incorporated all the family in the room. Even a small stipend was given for second-cousin Merida's unborn child. "–and the remainder of my estate to be divided equally between my daughters, Eileen and Dahlia, in trust for their children."

Adam hadn't been paying too much attention to the actual asset division, and so wasn't completely sure what remainder entailed. He felt his mother stiffen under his arm. "He left us the house," she whispered.

He instinctively turned to Hagatha. Her purple mountain majesty was red with spitting anger. The tirade that escaped her mouth stunned everyone to silence as she trantrumed like a two-year-old unaccustomed to the word *no.*

"Calm down, Aunt Agatha," Todd stated, firm against the tempest. "There are several things Dad set aside for you. You haven't been forgotten."

"Miserable Boy!" Hagatha spat. "You present the real will this instant. I'll see you disbarred for fraud and conspiracy to extort rightful property from elderly ladies!"

Waves of cousins attempted to distance themselves from Hagatha's epicenter, but there was little space in the living room left to go. Still, she shoved her way forward, parting bodies like the Red Sea, hands poised to grip Todd's throat. His blonde screamed and lashed out, obtaining a candlestick from a nearby shelf and striking a blow to Hagatha's skull.

The purple mountain majesty buckled from the force and crumbled to the floor, emitting a short-lived hiss like a punctured pipe.

The blonde dropped the candlestick and drew her hands up to hide her mouth. "Sorry Toddy."

Adam's mother released a sigh. "Thank Heaven for the kindness of strangers."

December sputtered out an inappropriate giggle and clapped her hands. "Encore!"

The room held itself agape. Everyone stood looking at each other, blinking dumbly. Petal rose from her seat and braved the walk to Agatha. She knelt, fingers probing the old woman's neck in search of a pulse. After a long moment, her fishing produced an answer. "Nope, she's still alive." She sounded so morbidly disappointed.

December bounced into the room, still clapping. "I said encore!"

Adam jumped in front of the neighbor. "Ah, there's, uh, dessert in the kitchen and if you'll give us a moment, Tess and I will find the key to the liquor cabinet."

CHAPTER SIX

Tuesday, 1:45 p.m.

"Aunt Agatha, no one is trying to steal anything from you," Adam's mother raised her voice above the old woman's caterwauling.

"Now, Sweetie, I know you're not guilty of that." Agatha dabbed at her pink eyes with a bright purple lady's handkerchief. "You're too sweet to be involved in such a conspiracy. I blame that worthless sister of yours. She did this to me, conspiring behind my back, convincing my invalid brother to leave everything to her."

Adam couldn't take it anymore. "Agatha, for Christ's sake, give it a fracking rest. When are you going to realize the world doesn't revolve around you?"

His mother ran her fingers through her hair, "Adam, I almost had her calmed down."

Hagatha stormed on, her words carrying refreshed poison. "You ungrateful, miserable louse! Your mother, God help her, deserves a better child than she got. You're just like that wretch of a husband of hers–"

"Enough!" Adam cringed reflexively at his mother's tone, the tone she used often against him when he stepped out of line. "Aunt

Agatha, I love you dearly. You're the matriarch of this family and I will always give you the respect you deserve, but if you continue to have the audacity to insult both my son and my husband to my face, wake or no wake, you can show yourself to the door."

Hagatha's red face puckered like a puffer fish. "You won't throw me out."

"Oh I most certainly will if you try me further. I will get the Marines involved if I have to, you understand me? You just poked a mother bear and I'll be damned if I'm going to let you hurt my son!"

Agatha blubbered and bubbled while mascara oozed down her cheeks in blood-like mudslides. Adam held his breath, stunned that the whole mess might soon be over. As his curse would have it, however, Hagatha was only getting started. "That Dahlia, she's convinced you too. She's turned you against me. I forgive you; you've always had more heart than brain."

Adam's mother sighed, throwing her hands in the air. "Agatha, you need help. You can't continue to live like this. This anger, this paranoia, this distrust...you've got to change or you're going to die a very lonely woman and there will be no grandchildren to look after you."

"More heart than brain." Hagatha repeated as if she hadn't heard a word and lay on the bed. Soon, a snore at decibels to rival a 747 reverberated off the walls of the ground floor guest room.

Adam touched his mother's elbow. "Come on, Mom. She's gonna be out for a while. Petal gave her enough sedative to knock out a horse."

"Yeah but we needed a dose to knock out a whale," December entered the room, giggling. "Or maybe a whole bunch of whales."

Adam's mother groaned, "Did Tess get the liquor cabinet opened yet?"

December nodded, "Todd's girlfriend used her nail file. I like her. She's blonde, and pretty. Oh and she's not all there upstairs if you get my meaning."

A sly smile crossed his mother's face, but she graciously ignored the comment about the blonde's intelligence. "Well, if the liquor cabinet is open, shall we go find the scotch and give Dad a proper send-off?"

They filed down the hallway, closing the door on the sleeping hag. Echoes of laughter drifted from the living room at the edge of spoken stories. Adam concentrated on breathing, allowing his shoulders to relax and the rage melt from his joints. With Hagatha out for the count, everyone was free of her oppressive presence, if only for a moment, and the house seemed brighter for it.

And after Hagatha's tantrum, Adam refused to feel guilt. He was officially done with her.

Tess pulled him aside before he could advance into the room. "We all knew Eileen was the only person who could calm her down. How'd it go?"

"Mom was amazing. It was wasted on Hagatha, but Mom was certainly amazing."

"Everyone is already in the gin and tonic...I'm concerned though. Have you seen the twins? They've completely disappeared, which means they're up to something."

December shuddered, "The spider one invited me to a party in his pants. Like that works."

Tess sneered, "Of course, because it's all about you."

Adam felt his tenuous calm ebbing away. "Tess, stop. December is here because she loved Grandpa Lum. Why can't you just put aside this bad past or vibe or whatever it is that's going on here and just accept her on those merits?"

Tess blinked and December looked puzzled. "Then you don't know?" his cousin asked.

"I don't know what?" The girls exchanged glances, volumes of unspoken conversation radioed between them. Confused, Adam thought hard about all the chatter he had overheard that day, searching for reason. "I don't know what?"

They began to giggle. Short bursts at first, then solid, tear-producing hearty chuckles that caused them to double over on themselves in a freak display of bonded sisterhood. Adam, dumb, watched the scene, frustrated at being the odd man out. Tess wiped her eyes, "I'm so sorry, December, I honestly thought he knew."

"You're not going to tell me either, are you?" Bitterness crept into his tone, which only incited coos and aws from the girls.

"What, you think we can't keep a secret?" December challenged, a sinister smile curling her mouth.

"Fine, whatever," Adam surrendered, throwing up his hands. "I'll go hunt the twins down."

They chased after him as he walked away. "No wait, don't be like that. We're coming too." Tess insisted, the memory of her laughter still evident in her voice.

He grabbed the tuna barge on route to the back door. Tess jumped in front of him to open it so he wouldn't have to juggle the casserole and the door knob. Adam muttered a thank you, but didn't make eye contact yet. He maneuvered down the steps, girls in tow, and walked with a heavy stride towards the barn.

Grandpa Lum's favorite meat was pork. There wasn't a time Adam's mother or her siblings could remember when they didn't have at least one sow in the pens near the stables. Adam approached the hogs carefully, armed with the knowledge that Grandpa didn't have enough stamina during his final days to work daily with the creatures. Adam wanted to be prepared if they had gone feral.

"I've been tending them," December answered his unvoiced question. "Mr. Kittridge has an appointment with the butcher for next month, and then it's sausage time."

"I wonder if Pig and Poke will notice they're getting their annual tuna casserole a little early this year," Tess stated, helping Adam flip the dish over the trough. The casserole slid out with little encouragement, slippery globs of cheese and fish splattering against the metal with a disappointing squish.

"Doubtful," Adam shook his head. "I don't think they were here for the last batch anyway. Grandpa had a white breed then, well two white sows and a black boar."

Pig and Poke trotted to the trough, fat and hairy. They were both red Hereford sows, the larger of the two weighing in around 620 pounds. The tuna casserole was quickly devoured and the pigs even rooted about for seconds. They were the only members of the family that ever expressed an appreciation for Hagatha's casserole.

"I hate pigs," Tess grumbled. "Disgusting creatures."

"Oh but the bacon. All this was worth it if only for the bacon." Adam turned, dish in hand, forgetting he wanted to be mad at them. "Wanna see the bats?" he offered.

"I thought we were looking for Chase and Chance."

"We are. I suspect they're behind the barn or they're up on the widow's walk. Since the hogs needed feeding anyway, I figured we could check while we're here."

"Good idea."

"We haven't been too successful with looking for things today," December said, her voice sounded far away.

Adam paused, absorbing the surrounding acreage. He wondered what would become of it all. The happiest days of his childhood was spent here, generally summers or school breaks when his father was overseas. If his mom and Aunt Dahlia agreed, perhaps he could move here, be a part of the land. He never was much of a city boy. "I found enough, I think," he breathed.

December crossed her eyes, "I meant the keys and stuff...what do you mean?"

"I found home."

December's vacant expression was back. "I didn't know the house was missing."

CHAPTER SEVEN

Tuesday, 2:30 p.m.

T HEY SPIED THE TWINS on the way back to the house. Chase and Chance lazed on the steep roof of the house astride the widow's walk, smoking. Adam exchanged a sharp look with Tess who grumbled something that ended with "stupid hoodlums."

December tugged at Adam's borrowed flannel, "Can we go get Teddy now? His time-out's over."

"You put your bear in time-out?" Adam didn't know what he disbelieved most, the fact that she was punishing a stuffed teddy bear, or the fact that it didn't surprise him like it should have.

She nodded. "He wouldn't let me have a drink from the flask earlier, which I thought was rude."

"Wackadoo," Tess sighed, "But about the drink..."

Adam placed the empty casserole boat on the kitchen counter and snatched a handful of chocolate chip cookies from a platter on the sink-board. Judging from the sounds emanating from the living room, Grandpa Lum's wake was in full force and the alcohol was flowing generously. The trio slipped in and spirited away a bottle of spiced rum. They would use the bottle to entice the twins to come in off of the roof, if it lasted that long.

They each shared a swig and a cookie before taking the series of long, Victorian staircases to the garret access. Opening the door to the widow's walk, they were assaulted by a breathing gale and a face full of foul-smelling smoke. "What the fuck, Chance!" Tess fumed, her fingers gripping her nose in a violent response to the stench.

"You're not smoking pot, Geniuses," Adam quipped. "That crap is catnip, remember?"

The twins shrugged and shared another hit. "Doesn't-matter, it's-still-got-a-numbing-effect." Chase mumbled, not bothered by the criticism.

Chance rubbed his face the way Sauerkraut had in the garden. "Did you know we're closer to the sun up here?"

"Yeah, and some days the sun reaches all the way to the ground," Adam leaned against the railing, offering the last two cookies to the potheads who snatched them up greedily. "This whole scenario has the makings of a classic Greek tragedy."

"If I push him off, do you think he'll fly?" December asked, wiping her mouth on her sleeve before returning the bottle to Tess.

"Come on Icharus," Tess waved the rum under their noses. "The sun will set you on fire if you fly too close."

"Yeah, why don't we go down and behave like a normal family?" Adam suggested. "We're missing out on the stories."

"Who-cares-about-old-people-stories?" Chase asked.

Tess folded her arms. "You do. The Amanda topic might get raised."

He frowned, "You-said-you-wouldn't-say-nothing."

Chance looked like he was preparing to leap off the roof to his death, "You jackass! How does Tess know about Amanda?"

"What, you missed it the first time she said anything?" Adam reminded them, "C'mon. You know Tess is a human Wikipedia."

"Now that nickname I like." Tess smirked and wagged a finger at the twins. "So you two are coming down, right?"

The twins stood up, slipping as they tried to pull their pants up. Adam leaned over the walk railing to offer a hand and helped them both over. They escaped the wind, retreating to the warm indoors and the myriad of creaky staircases. "Say wouldn't it be something, Tess, if our mothers allowed us to, I don't know, turn this into a bed and breakfast maybe?" Adam sound-boarded off the walls before they reached the first floor.

"Where'd that come from?" Tess grabbed his arm to stop his advance. "You're using your serious voice."

"Maybe I am serious. Maybe...I don't know." He looked at his cousins' faces, attempting to ascertain their opinion from their puzzled expressions. "It's just, Mom's keeping our lives together fine, but we haven't exactly set down roots and I'm already out of college. Dad's been in one tour after the other from the time I could remember. Aunt Dahlia and Uncle Curtis seem to be okay with their furniture business, and they don't really need this place."

Tess folded her arms and glared at him, her right eyebrow arched suspiciously. "So because you don't have roots, my mom and dad should give up rights to the house?"

"No!" he back-peddled from the assumption. "I didn't mean it like that, honest. I meant partners. This place needs a ton of updating and some regular maintenance. Mom and I could run the place easily, I think, and with your marketing degree and the twins, uh, need for gainful employment, I mean, don't you think?"

"Adam, you're not making any sense," she shivered as if every joint in her body reacted to his suggestion. "And it's not our decision anyway."

"Fine, forget I brought it up," he replied, feeling foolish. He trod down the rest of the stairs and attempted to regain composure.

"Why-not-have-a-B'n'B?" It was Chase's turn to stop. Adam remembered seeing this expression years ago, the day they discovered the candy store in town. "Why-not?" he repeated, his words laced with hope.

Tess blinked at them both, "Why would you even find this remotely appealing?"

Chase shuffled his feet and nudged his brother. The twins had a secret, unspoken argument before Chance coughed. "Look, things around our neighborhood aren't exactly looking up. Uncle Lum wanted us to straighten ourselves out, but if we don't have somewhere to go, we may never be able to walk away from it."

"I'll be damned all to Hell," Tess expressed, shock blanching her face. "Those words actually came outta your mouth."

Adam felt just as surprised. His mother's cousin's twin pothead boys just made sense and expressed concern that perhaps their lives really did need a new direction. The apocalypse was happening and the epicenter was right in Grandpa Lum's house. "Um, okay, well how about we get Teddy out of time-out, and then raise a glass or two with everyone in the living room, and then if we're drunk enough to talk about it, we'll ask for Mom and Dahlia's opinion. Fair deal?"

December folded her hands as if in prayer. "See what happens when Mr. Kittridge's stinkin' sister keeps her big, fat, stupid nose out of things?"

Tess smirked, "What, the end of the world?"

Chuckling, Adam turned to the redhead, "So where's your bear?"

"I left him under the cellar staircase," she replied. "He should feel good and apologetic by now."

CHAPTER EIGHT

Tuesday, 2:45 p.m.

"WE'LL MEET YOU IN THE LIVING ROOM," Tess announced and grabbed the neckline of the twin closest to her. "I don't see the need for five of us to fetch a stupi – er – stuffed bear." She dragged Chase and Chance from the hallway.

"Ladies first," Adam opened the door for December and turned the light on.

She slipped passed him, her footsteps gentle on the staircase. "Did you really mean it?"

"Mean what?" he followed, closing the door loosely behind them. He didn't figure they'd be here that long.

She turned at the base of the steps, catching his gaze. Light danced in her eyes, bright as sapphires. Crazy was definitely a weakness. "Did you really mean you want to open a bed and breakfast?"

"Oh that," he sighed, sticking his hands in his pockets. His fingertips touched the catnip, a not-so-subtle reminder that the weed needed to be disposed of. "Yeah, I guess. I mean, Mom and I talked about it before, back when I was still in high school. Open up a bed and breakfast, sell veggies on the side. In the back of mind, I always thought of Grandpa's house when we discussed it. Why?"

She chewed on her lip, a decision to be made coloring the expression on her face. "I know I'm not much of a people person, and maybe not someone to have around at a B and B, but I'd kinda like to be a part of it anyway..."

He considered her for a long time while hope and innocence flooded her eyes. He liked her, her strange communication skills and her occasional crude behavior he found endearing. "It's not a bed and breakfast yet, so the whole plan might be moot. But, if you could put up with our crazy bunch, I wouldn't mind keeping you around."

Her nose wrinkled at his comment and she whirled about, diving beneath the staircase for Teddy.

The cellar door flew open and a screaming yellow furball sailed through the air over the banister. Adam ducked before two pairs of sharp paws nailed his head. "Addy, Dear," Hagatha's shrill voice raped his eardrums. "See how you like being locked in the trunk."

"Agatha?" The door slammed shut and the locking mechanism slid into place. Adam sprinted up the stairs and pounded on the door. "Agatha!"

December let out an inappropriate giggle. "You sound like Fred from that caveman cartoon."

He ignored the comment and slammed his fist against the stubborn door repeatedly. "Agatha, you miserable...What the hell!"

His crazy companion sighed, and pulled the knit cap from her skull. Free of their prison, strawberry curls exploded around her face. December sank in the middle of the slab floor, crossing her legs with her bear in her lap. "Adam."

"What!" he barked, instantly regretful. "I'm sorry, I didn't mean that tone."

She cocked her head, curious, as if meeting him for the first time. "Adam, sit."

Her voice had a strange calming effect and he pulled himself away from his frustration to follow her simple instructions, careful to leave enough space between them so as not to make her uncomfortable. The patchwork bear showed no signs of being remorseful for his unacceptable behavior. "What does–" he wondered how to pronounce the words that he remembered were stitched to Teddy's bottom, "–pawg moe thone mean?"

She giggled again and bared the bear's behind to show off the stitching. "Poeg meh hone," she corrected, pointing out each word corresponding with her pronunciation. "It's Irish Gaelic. It means: kiss my ass."

He laughed from his gut until his sides hurt. "Bloody brilliant," he managed between breaths. He envisioned all ways he could slip that into conversation, and almost all of those conversations had Hagatha at the receiving end.

"Don't move," December whispered, breaking his reverie.

"Why? Is there a black widow?" he twitched at the thought.

"No. Worse." She pointed at the shadows near the apothecary drawers to a pair of glowing eyes. The darkness growled.

"Shit, it's Sauerkraut," he whispered, frozen to his patch of floor.

As if responding to her name, Sauerkraut crept from her cover, moving towards them.

December whispered, "Stay put. I'll get a pot-bear."

"No need," he fumbled for the catnip in his pocket. "I've been meaning to dispose of this somehow."

"It'll only work for about 15 minutes," December warned.

"It'll be enough." He reached out with the weed displayed in his open hand. "I hope."

The yellow cat stopped and sniffed, her little, black-speckled nose flaring. Sauerkraut purred, loud and proud, and she collapsed to the ground, rolling onto her side, squeezing her eyes.

"No wonder he horded the stuff," Adam exclaimed. He watched the cat drool for a moment, until he became aware of December's proximity. She was close enough to touch for the first time that day.

"Adam, I like you." She placed her bear down and inched forward.

The mood changed. The cellar was warmer. She looked different, her curls spiraling wild atop her head. There was an aura of confidence about her, a sense of urgency. "I like you, too."

"I have issues," she drew closer.

"Yes, you've said." *So this is it. She's going to kiss me.*

"I mean it. I have serious mental problems."

He could feel her breath, taste the rum and chocolate in the space between them. "I know."

"I'm not normal." She paused, her lips close to his.

"Who the hell wants normal?"

Their kiss was the first first kiss that ever felt natural. It was something he experienced, driving all thought from his mind. He didn't hear the door creak open, didn't notice his cousins descend the staircase, didn't register that Tess cleared her throat.

"Ah, shit, I should've known you were lying about her not being your girl." Chance snorted.

Adam didn't feel embarrassed that their kiss was interrupted. And judging December's reaction, neither did she. Her eyes narrowed at Chance, "Póg mo thóin."

Adam suppressed his outburst of laughter and rose from the floor, offering December a hand up, and to his surprise, she accepted.

Tess clicked her teeth, "Fetching the bear, eh? Was this the plan before Hagatha locked you in here?"

Adam merely grinned, "Come on; let's see if we can't kill a witch."

"Seriously?" December beamed with hope.

He shrugged, "If there's anything I learned today, it's that anything can happen."

CHAPTER NINE

Tuesday, 3:00 p.m.

THE SITUATION IN THE LIVING ROOM BECAME VOLATILE. With everyone corralled without an exit, Agatha pushed buttons. Red-faced, puffing air, she was a steam engine of accusations. Todd appeared to be the only one unaffected by her tirade, laughing whenever her pudgy finger pointed his direction. Adam braced himself for the full wrath. He was as ready as he would ever be.

"And you!" Hagatha seethed, her attention directed now at Tess. "For all your expensive, fancy college degrees, you can't even land a man."

Adam could feel Tess stiffen through the space between them. "Look who's calling the kettle black, Ms. Pot!" she retaliated.

"You're probably one of them lezbeans, ain't you, Bessie dear?"

Curtis got up from his chair, "That's enough, Agatha."

"Oh sit back down, Curdle. You ain't even a man," Hagatha reared. "A man wouldn't raise his daughter to be a lezbean."

"Stop it you miserable, fucking bitch!" Tess screamed, wagging her fist in Hagatha's face. "First off, my name is Tess. Tess! With a T not a B. Second, you're the only person here in it for her own fucking gain. The rest of us actually loved Grandpa Lum, and we're here as a family to send him off in a proper fashion. You? You're just a waste of a grunt and nine months!"

"How dare you!" Hagatha sputtered, a spray of saliva spewed into the room. "I gave the best years of my life tending to my invalid brother and I didn't see any of his ungrateful children or his useless grandchildren lift a single finger to help him."

December pulled a set of keys from Agatha's large sack-like purse. "If your car keys are locked in your trunk, why didn't you just open it with your spare set?"

Adam stared at the keys, murder outflanking the rest of the thoughts in his mind.

Shock blockaded the reason from the room. Hagatha turned a deeper shade of scarlet, "You little thief! You hand me my purse this instant. Todd, do something useful with your law degree and arrest her!"

Todd poured himself another shot of whiskey, "Yeah, good luck with that."

"Oh I see. You're all trying to kill me. First you lock my keys in the trunk so I can't leave, then you hire that two-bit prostitute to murder me with a candlestick, and then when that didn't work, you slip me an overdose of heroine to make it look like I'm a drug addict. Well I'm on to you!" the old woman spit as she stomped off to the kitchen. They could hear her fumble with the wall phone in an attempt to dial out.

"What happened when we were locked in the cellar?" Adam asked his mother as she crossed the room.

"Oh, you know, the usual rubbish," she sighed and straightened his collar.

I should've put a pillow over her face when she started snoring, he thought. "Was she always that mean?"

"For as long as I can remember, only never to me, and I never understood why. Oh, she would insult my intelligence, but the way she treated me was almost as if she actually respected me."

Todd's glass was empty again, and he reached for a bottle. "You made a necklace for Mom one time, I think for Mother's Day or something, out of handmade paper beads. You know, the kind you make by rolling up pieces of cut-up magazine pictures. You were so excited bringing it home from school that you rushed in the house to show everyone."

"Yeah, I remember the necklace, but nothing else."

"Aunt Agatha was sitting at the kitchen table talking with Dad, and Mom ran from the room crying because of something Agatha said. And you had that necklace in your hands, proudly waving it in the air. 'Look, look what I made!' you said. And Agatha took it from you, thinking you made it for her."

"You think that's why she likes me? Because I let her have Mom's present?"

Todd took a long sip from his glass. "Stranger things have been known to happen. She never had any love for Mom. It's one of the reasons we didn't see much of her growing up. Dad wasn't going to force Mom to deal with her."

Quiet fell on the gathering like a damp blanket, heavy and burdensome. Agatha's harsh voice could be heard from the kitchen. She was arguing with a 9-1-1 operator.

December rifled through the sack-purse and eventually produced a checkbook. From its fold, she retrieved a picture, faded yellow with age. She exhaled, slowly. "I know why she's a bitch," she announced.

She had everyone's attention, but she didn't act as if she noticed. "Oh, what's your theory, December?" Adam's mother asked.

The redhead looked up from the photograph. She looked older somehow, caught in a tangled web of emotion. "This is a picture of the man she wanted to marry. He went to fight in Germany. He never came home. His name I think...Ellis, Ellery? Ellery Stickney."

The family spent the next few moments exchanging puzzled glances. December had almost made a human of Agatha.

Almost.

December tucked the photo in her pocket and threw the purse down as Hagatha stormed back into the living room. The old woman was as smug as a pig in mud. "The cops are coming to arrest you, Whore," she announced to Todd's companion. "Attempted murder. They might work out a deal with you if you name all your co-conspirators."

The blonde was Bambi in headlights. She appealed quickly to Todd who assured her not to worry. "You're fine Cinnamon. It was a clear case of self-defense and I doubt anyone here but Agatha would say otherwise."

"You sure Toddy?" she twirled a strand of hair between slender fingers.

"Of course." He cast Agatha a long-wise look, his eyes like steel. "She doesn't have a legal foot to stand on."

Sauerkraut launched into the room, a spiky ball of yellow fur and claws, and sank her teeth into Agatha's ankle. Adam's family broke like billiard balls, scattering away from the frantic old woman with the new, feline leg-attachment. Adam watched with a mixture of morbid curiosity and sheer delight as Agatha twisted and kicked and screamed. Blood pooled on her shoes as her leg leaked thick, red rivers. She reached for the fireplace poker and in a move straight out of a Three Stooges episode, she aimed the dangerous end at Sauerkraut and swung.

The cat, maybe sensing a life-threatening strike from a wrought-iron instrument of death, disengaged at the speed of light and disappeared.

Agatha didn't have time to alter course. She stuck herself with the poker.

There was a delay in her reaction, as if shock and pain occurred in separate time zones. Petal, ever the nurse in the family, sprang to action, hurdling past nonreactive family to administer first-aid. She barked instructions at the old woman, and called for help when Agatha tried to fight her off.

Adam saw his mother pour a shot of whiskey and slam it back before she leaped to Petal's defense. "Agatha, we can't help you if you don't calm down," she shouted.

"The cat's a demon from HELL!" Agatha cried out, still clutching the poker in her hands.

"It's not the cat this time, Agatha, it's you. You stabbed yourself with a fireplace poker. Do you understand that you need medical attention?" Adam's mother shrieked.

"Demon from HELL! Demon from HELL!" She blanched as she chanted, her wild eyes searching for something and not finding.

"Agatha, I really need you to calm down," Petal grabbed the woman's face, trying to make eye contact. "I really need you to breathe. Deeply. One. Two."

"Demon from HELL!" Agatha let go of the poker and it crashed to the floor, shredding what was left of her skin. She then clenched her pudgy fingers into a fist and slugged Petal, knocking her out cold.

"Shit!" Adam dove to catch Petal before she hit the ground, looking up in time to catch his mother – *his mother!* – smack the hag square on the cheek.

For a brief, blissful moment, it looked like the slap might've worked. Agatha puffed and sucked in a deep breath, but alas, she was just gearing up for another act of her tantrum play. "From HELL!" Hagatha bellowed, shoving her niece aside. She tore through the room, bowling over those unfortunate enough to get in her way. All the while, blood pumped from her torn leg at rapid intervals, baptizing furniture and family alike as she retreated down the hallway like a loosed banshee.

A pout hovered over December's lips. "Did anyone catch that on their camera? I'd pay money to see that again. With popcorn."

Adam had to agree with her.

CHAPTER TEN

Tuesday, 3:45 p.m.

THEY HADN'T HEARD A PEEP FROM HAGATHA since the cat attack. Petal came to and insisted that the paramedics be called. Not a single person in the room wanted to do it, so Cinnamon, as the odd-man-out, dialed 9-1-1. "To make sure Petal's okay," she specified.

Everyone agreed with that motivation.

"Does anyone know where she ended up?" Petal asked after the call was placed, an ice pack pressed to her right eye.

"I'll-follow-the-blood," Chase offered.

"Be careful Boysh. She's a bit unshtable." Sissy warned her sons over her gin and tonic. "Oh and make shure she shtays put when you find her. Don't let her outta your shightsh."

"Lock her up, got it." Chance replied, tugging his pants up as they sauntered after Hagatha's bloody trail.

Uncle Curtis wrapped an arm around Tess. "Are you okay, Honey? She was unusually cruel."

Adam could tell the answer to that just by looking at her, but Tess usually lied to her parents about how she felt. "Oh yeah. That old bat couldn't injure me if she tried."

"You don't sound okay," he probed her further. "You sound like you're about ready to cry."

"I don't cry, Dad. You know that." Tess sniffed and turned away. The corners of her eyes turned pink like a barometer forecasting a coming storm. "Don't worry about me. Just look after Mom. She's been staring out the window since Agatha locked Adam in the cellar."

Adam examined his borrowed slacks, dismayed at the fresh coating of blood. Fate wasn't entirely done dishing out her special brand of torture, or so he believed. December waved Teddy's butt in his face, soliciting a laugh. In that one, frivolous move, she chased his bad Karma from his thoughts.

Outside, the sound of sirens announced the coming emergency medical team. "They're in for one helluva ride," Todd muttered. He pushed the blinds back on the window to peek outside. "I'll greet them. See if I can direct them through all the parked cars. Let them know what's going on. Recommend a good therapist to deal with the aftermath of Agatha."

December shivered. "Therapy isn't for the weak," she muttered, her voice speaking through layers of experience. "People would be better off hugging a teddy bear."

Adam's mother raised a hand to her neck and rubbed, audibly popping tension loose. She sighed, "I don't know about you folks, but I'm peckish. I'm gonna break out the leftovers, if anybody wants any. It's probably best if we stay out of the way of the emergency crew anyway." She headed for the kitchen and the room emptied behind her.

Acetaminophen wearing thin, the dull throb returned to Adam's head. Agatha certainly had a lot to answer for. Adam pinched the bridge of his nose and exhaled. Tess pushed another capsule in his hand. "I told you to take two earlier," she chided him.

"I know. I just hate taking pills. I would rather have another drink."

Todd led the way for a team of emergency medical technicians. "Sissy, did you see where the twins went?"

"Nope." Sissy shifted in the armchair and hollered towards the hallway, "Chaysh! Chansh! Come get the para – hic – medicsh!"

Chance appeared, "Hey Todd, she's locked in the cellar. We haven't heard a word from her in a while."

The techs exchanged glances and maneuvered the furniture-cluttered room towards the cellar. Adam recognized Oscar Lindsey, the son of the pharmacist in town, and they nodded a greeting to each other in passing. Oscar received Agatha-scoldings before, so Adam was pretty confident that the team knew who they were up against and were as prepared as they could possibly be.

Tess nudged Adam, reminding him of the pill in his hand. "Take it," she ordered, offering her flask to wash it down.

"I shouldn't mix–" he started.

"Then take it dry, what do I care," Tess interrupted. "Or don't take it at all, but I'd better not hear you complaining about your headache later."

Chase burst into the room, pulling his pants up. "Hagatha's-dead!"

Adam choked on the pill, coughing it free from his throat and projecting it across the room. "Can't be," he coughed again. "She's actually dead? As in, no longer breathing, rotten soul collected, dead?"

"Yippee!" December flipped Teddy up in the air, where the stuffed bear could execute a perfect triple somersault. "It's a great day for America everybody!"

The paramedics filed back in. Oscar peeled off a latex glove while his comrades saw to Petal's eye. "Adam, good to see you."

"Agatha's dead?" Shock swept the headache from the back of his eyes. "I'm sorry Oscar, yeah, it's great to see you. Especially under these circumstances, I mean if Hagatha's really kicked it."

He nodded, a giddy grin plastered to his face. "There was absolutely nothing we could do to save her I admit. Not a one."

Petal shoved the medics aside, a dark circle evident around her eye. "You're joking!"

"Nope, no joke," Oscar crossed his heart and held up two fingers in the Boy Scout salute. "I promise you I would never lie about something so critical. You have my sincerest congratulations."

A minor explosion happened in the far corner as a champagne cork sailed into the ceiling. Todd poured frothy bubbles from a large champagne bottle into a waiting teacup. "Calls for a celebration don't you think? Drink up!"

"What caused her death?" The question escaped like an avalanche from Adam's mouth.

Oscar shrugged, "That's not my call to make. I know that her heart has stopped beating and that life has left her eyes. That's enough for me. I've radioed the coroner's office. They may want to do something about her. They may not. They'll let you know."

Todd interrupted, "Who cares? Champagne, Oscar?"

Oscar laughed, "Tempting, but we gotta hit the road. It was nice seeing everyone again. I'm sorry about Lum. He was a great man."

"Well stop by when your shift is over," Todd said. "I have a feeling we'll be here for a good part of the night. I may even send the twins out for a couple keggers."

A mixture of delight and hope washed across Tess's face. "I don't believe it. Do you think she could've bled out that quickly?"

"I wouldn't have thought so, but anything's possible right?" Adam watched a trickle of family working its way back into the living room, food piled on paper plates. The shadows of the house disappeared completely. Laughter and joy filled the empty spaces and some spontaneous dancing ensued between spouses.

And Sissy started singing, surprisingly on key. "Theresh a bright morning coming..."

Dave, Jim, and Petal joined in, "Coming one bright day."

"O there's a bright morning coming one day," piped up Curtis and Tess.

Everyone stopped eating and drinking and started singing, rafter-shaking loud. Adam felt the pictures vibrate on the walls as feet stomped and hands clapped. "There's a bright morning coming, sending stars and moon a-runnin'."

December danced over to Adam, "That was one of Mr. Kittridge's favorites. O song of summer glory, the winter's gone away."

Adam reached over and snatched off her knit cap, exposing her curls, "There's a knit cap a comin'."

She made a face, stuck out her tongue, and tossed her bear up for another somersault. "Coming one bright day."

The warmth of the room and the spirit of the moment melted the stress from his soul.

CHAPTER ELEVEN

Tuesday, 4:30 p.m.

OFFICER DANNY TRENCHER ARRIVED with the coroner, but that did little to dampen the spirits of the Kittridge clan. Adam thought it tragic that no one shed a tear for Agatha. He couldn't summon any emotion for her either. In fact, not one happy story could be shared among the family. Agatha didn't once show any kindness towards anyone. As a result, no one showed any kindness to her.

Except December.

After the initial celebrations, December pulled the photo out of her pocket and tucked herself into the corner with her bear. Curious, Adam approached her, still cautious of her aversion to human contact. He returned her cap and parked himself on the floor beside her. "What's up?"

She held on the photo for a long moment before speaking, her voice meek and tenuous. "Remember when I told you that I have some serious problems?"

"Yeah. Remember when I said who the hell wants normal?" Adam was concerned that maybe she'd decided it was a bad move to hook up.

She sneered, teasing him, "Yes, I remember."

"Sooo, what's really up here?" Adam probed again.

She didn't answer him, simply handed him the photo.

The gentleman in the picture was a handsome, strong-looking individual in a U.S. Army uniform. Worn and faded, the image spoke to years of being fawned at, folded up, and stuffed in wallets. Adam absently turned the photograph over, expecting to read the faded information that December had found earlier. There was nothing there.

December looked fearful, as if expecting an aggressive reaction from him. He was too confused to figure out why. "You gave us a name earlier, and a history..."

She nodded, taking staccato breaths. "Ellery Stickney. He went to Germany in World War II. He never came back to her. She believed he died there. Agatha died with him. Hagatha was born then."

Adam regarded her, unsure what to think. "Okay, what? You worried you're broken and will turn bitter like Agatha?"

She shook her head, stroking the ears of her bear. "No, that's not the point you're missing."

"What then? I'd rather you tell me than keep it buried inside."

"I know things. Not like Tess does. Tess knows a lot of things because she studies and reads and argues a lot. The things I know, I know because...because..." She released a breath and looked away.

Adam didn't understand. He tried to, but he just didn't get what she might have been hinting at. Tess tapped him on the shoulder. "Officer Trencher is ready for you."

"Oh?"

"Yeah, he wants to ask you about the keys and the trunk."

"Okay thanks." He got up with reluctance and walked upstairs to the sitting room on the second floor landing. He tapped at the door before entering. "Officer Trencher?"

"Have a seat, Son."

"Sure." Adam sat across from Trencher, mind still trying to work out the December puzzle. It took him a moment to realize he'd been asked something. "I'm sorry, what was that?"

Trencher chuckled, "Been a long day, eh?"

"Yeah. You know I started off on the wrong foot with Hagatha today." Adam saw no reason to avoid the interrogation. Besides, he didn't have anything to hide.

"Hagatha? Nice."

"Yeah, well, to know her is to hate her."

"So, something was mentioned about locking her keys in the trunk?" Trencher asked, back to business. "About what time was that?"

"Just after 10, just after I arrived this morning."

"Ah." He wrote something down in his notebook, and then tapped his chin with his pencil. "God, you know I hate this, right?"

"Uh?"

"I knew the old bat, too, you know? Well, I guess knew is a relative term. She's verbally assaulted me on more than one occasion. Every time I tried to actually write her up for something, she managed to scare me out of it." Trencher shook his head. "I hate like hell investigating this because I could care less if anybody killed her."

Adam nodded. He knew the feeling. "So, look, I don't know who if anyone actually would've killed her. We're talking about my family after all, but really the only time period I think you need to worry about is after, oh, 3:00 maybe? That's when Sauerkraut, er Lum's feral barn mouser, attached herself to Hagatha's leg and Hagatha reached for the fireplace poker."

"That must've been a sight," the officer looked amused, wistful at the idea even.

"We tried to get her to calm down after she stuck herself, but she punched Petal in the face and ran down the hall. We debated calling the paramedics, but Petal being a nurse insisted and Sissy sent the twins to keep her contained."

"How does December Ashby figure into all this?"

Adam bristled. *What is he implying?* "Grandpa Lum treated her like family. She came here to pay her respects."

"Is that what she told you?" Trencher looked sincere.

"No, it's what my mom told me." *Stick that in your pipe, Copper.*

He leaned forward in his seat, "When Ms. Kittridge called to report the assault, she named December Ashby, Cinnamon Monroe, Dahlia and Curtis Archer, and you. Now I don't have any evidence of the Archers ever remotely acting against Ms. Kittridge, and Miss Monroe isn't too sharp upstairs, but this is the first she's ever encountered that strong a force of nature. Which leaves you and Miss Ashby."

"It leaves us?" Adam jumped up and began to pace. "Horse-shit!"

"Now, calm down Mr. Bingham. Miss Ashby has a history of malicious acts against Ms. Kittridge." The officer tapped his notebook, applying emphasis to his words. "Joyriding Ms. Kittridge's Cadillac–"

"–because Grandpa told her to."

"–sticking sugar in the tank–"

"–which she never did because Grandpa hated it when Hagatha stayed the night, so I'd assume Hagatha invented the story."

"–stalking Ms. Kittridge in town–"

"–the other way around actually. December actually lives in this neck of the woods and so has business being in town. Hagatha bitched all the time that there was nothing downtown she wanted or needed that she couldn't just as easily get from her own local Wal-Mart. What's to understand here?"

Trencher's stare was intense, harsh. "Are you in love with Miss Ashby?"

Adam's blood boiled, molten lava in his veins. He couldn't believe his ringing ears. This line of questioning was a study of the ridiculous. "What? I just met the girl."

"But you're sweet on her, aren't you?"

Adam unclenched his fists. "That's officially none of your business."

"And do you feel the need to protect or shield Ms. Ashby?"

Adam folded his arms, feeling fire brand the muscles beneath his skin. "What I feel is that this conversation is over. If it isn't, too damned bad 'cause I ain't saying anything else to you without a lawyer present."

Trencher scribbled some more notes in his little book. "Thank you, Mr. Bingham. You may go."

Adam quick-marched out the room and down the stairs to find Todd. He was in the kitchen with his sisters, deep in conversation. "Uncle Todd, I need a lawyer, in fact we all do, 'cause that stupid cop thinks someone actually murdered Agatha."

"Hey whoa, grab the reigns Kiddo," Todd straightened, "Danny's a decent cop. He's doing his job. What's going on?"

"What's going on is that he's a complete jackass. He just asked me if I'm in love with December and I want to know what that's gotta do with Hagatha's death."

Todd looked confused, "He what?"

"He said that when Agatha called, the people she reported were your girlfriend, Aunt Dahlia and Uncle Curtis, December and me."

"Todd, do something," the sisters said in unison.

"Eileen, Dahlia, it's okay. I'll take care of it. Danny Trencher's a good man, there's no need to panic." Todd turned and grabbed Adam elbow as he left the kitchen. Adam shook his arm free, frustrated. Todd paused. "You okay?"

"Yeah, sorry, I'm just...yeah, fine." He lied. He wasn't fine, but he knew it wasn't Todd's fault.

His uncle wasn't fooled. His mouth curled up in a suspicious smirk. "Well, I told you I'll take care of it, but I gotta ask. You and December?"

"Maybe. Is it really pertinent?"

"No," Todd laughed and clapped him on the shoulder. "I just wanted to know."

CHAPTER TWELVE

Tuesday, 5:00 p.m.

ADAM WATCHED TODD CLIMB THE STAIRCASE, an empty pit gnawing at his gut. No one killed Hagatha, he knew this. Officer Trencher was just doing his job, he knew this too. The question was: why was he so steamed?

December wasn't in the corner anymore. A quick search revealed she was gone again. "Damn," he breathed.

"Adam, where'sh your mother?" Sissy staggered towards him, barely missing the sideboard in her list. "I have a queshtion for her."

"She's in the kitchen with Dahlia."

"Who ish?" she blinked.

"My mother."

Sissy looked around and shook her head. "I don't know where your mother ish."

He pinched the bridge of his nose and choked down laughter. "She's in the kitchen."

"Oh," she nodded. "I have a queshtion for her."

Adam stepped aside, "Well, she's in there, with Dahlia."

"Who ish?"

God, it's like talking to a water-wheel. "Hey Mom!" he called. "Sissy has a question for you."

His mother appeared in the doorway, wiping her hands on a dishtowel, the faint odor of reheated potluck drifting about her. "Sissy, you doin' okay Hun'?"

"Oh, Eily, you have the besht timing. I have a queshtion for you."

"Whatchya need?"

Sissy giggled. "No that'sh not the queshtion."

"Are you looking for the twins?" his mother offered after a moment of swaying.

"What, my boysh? No my boysh are –" she threw her arm in a wide arc to gesture towards the hall and threw her balance off enough to stagger in place, "– well my boysh were over there shomewhere."

"When was the last time you had anything to eat, Sissy?"

"I had two three petuniash and a piccolo."

It hurt. Adam fought the laughter and searing pain blurred his vision. He didn't know how much longer he could hold out.

"–a piccolo?" his mother was asking.

Sissy pet her cousin's face, "No, dear, I'm not allergic to pickle loaf."

"Focus!" she begged. "What did you need to ask me?"

A thousand roman candles exploded in her drunken expression, "Eily! I have a queshtion for you!"

"Yes you said. What was the question, can you remember?" Adam couldn't tell if his mother was speaking slowly through frustration or a true desire to be helpful. Either way, he felt a nomination for sainthood was in order.

"Nope, I remember I was shupposhed to ashk you shomething and now I can't remember what it wash."

"Well, why don't you let Adam go by then, huh Sissy, and..."

"No wait, I know!" Sissy looked furtively about as much as her alcoholic swagger allowed before shouting her whisper at the top of her lungs. "Do you know where that misherable bitch of a hag ish?"

Adam couldn't hide his laughter anymore. It burst from his gut with volcanic fury, and his mother shot him a look. "Agatha's gone, Sissy. Why don't you come into the kitchen and get a drink of water, huh?"

"Okay, Eily. Shay, I've got a queshtion..."

Adam stumbled away holding his sides as tears leaked from his eyes. He could always count on Sissy having her share of alcohol, at least at family gatherings. According to Chance, there was never any alcohol in their house and Sissy was the prime example of the world's most perfect mother. Nobody dealt with Hagatha without falling off the wagon though. A quick assessment of the living room proved that the whole family imbibed liberally. At this rate, they'd all have to stay until the sober sun dethroned the drunken moon.

Officer Trencher descended the staircase, white as freshly bleached sheets. He walked with a zombie stride, shifting and shuffling heavily. At the foot of the stairs, the officer dropped his notepad, but he didn't lean over to pick it up. He simply craned his head towards the second floor and stared.

Todd must've done a number on him. Adam wiped his eyes and reached out to pick up the notepad. He had to force it into the officer's hand. "Hey, you okay in there?"

Trencher didn't respond.

"Officer Trencher?"

He turned and viewed the room with vacant attention, as if he was an alien in his own skin. Todd materialized at the edge of the landing, his smug smile lacking fortitude. "Danny, it's okay. None of us knew."

"Well obviously somebody knew." He pointed to the second floor parlor.

"Okay, so maybe one person knew. That doesn't mean the rest of us did."

"Yeah, well, it'll be public record now, won't it Todd?"

The lawyer shrugged, "If it becomes public record, it won't be because of me."

"And I'm just supposed to take your word for that?" The conversation felt foreign and dangerous to Adam, as if it was destined to be redacted from a top secret file and buried in a redundant government warehouse. He couldn't move in case the situation went sideways and they noticed he'd overheard the whole exchange.

Something sinister flashed in Todd's eyes. "Danny, we grew up together. Do you honestly believe I'd feed you to the wolves?"

"No I guess not. Thanks for everything, Todd. I'll be on my way." The officer paused and flashed a worried look at December as she emerged on the landing with her bear tucked under her chin. "Just keep her away from me."

"You have my word."

Adam watched the officer retreat into the crowd of Kittridges and slink through the front door like a kicked puppy. When he thought it was safe, he wheeled on his uncle. "Tell me what that was all about. I'm not gonna have to worry about getting abducted by spies in the middle of the night, am I?"

Todd shook his head, "No, at least I don't think so."

"What got him so spooked, then?"

"Wish I could tell you, Buddy, but I gave my word." He nodded towards December and emphasized the movement by bringing a finger to his lips. "Damn I wish I could tell you."

December didn't seem to have the same fragility lingering around her. She wiggled her finger at Adam, suggesting he climb the staircase, which he did. "Your uncle said you stood up for me," she smiled brightly. "No one but Mr. Kittridge ever stood up for me before."

"And why wouldn't I stand up for you? I don't want to sound like a broken record, but I thought we already established that I don't mind your particular brand of crazy."

"We did," she hugged her bear tight. "Doesn't mean I'm used to it yet."

"So tell me you know what that was all about. Why Officer Trencher looked like a man at the gallows?" he pleaded.

He watched her smile fade. "Yes...about that."

"Wait, you can't tell me either?"

She shook her head, "I can, but there's something else we need to talk about first."

"About the picture you stole from Hagatha's purse?"

"Yes, no, wait I didn't steal anything!" she protested. "I just borrowed it for a bit. I've already put it back."

"All right, you didn't steal it."

She grabbed his sleeve and dragged him across the creaky floorboards. Adam found himself back in the parlor. "I know things because they talk to me," she blurted, hiding her face behind her bear.

"Things *talk* to you?" *Does not compute.* "Can you...elaborate maybe?"

Her heavy sigh sounded like it came from the bear. "Hand me something, anything, like your wallet."

Adam reached inside his pocket and withdrew his wallet, depositing it in her extended, open hand.

She dropped her bear and cradled his worn, leather wallet. For a moment, he thought she forgot he was there. She breathed, raising her misty eyes to meet his. "Your dad gave you this wallet before his second tour in Afghanistan."

How the fuck does she know that? "Yes, I guess he did. H–"

"He spent a lot of time choosing this wallet, did you know that?" she interrupted. "He stood at the display counter for over an hour, debating between leather and canvas, bi-folds and tri-folds, blacks and browns. Part of it was the actual wallet itself. Deep down though, deep down your father was worried that he might not come home. Anyone can die in battle, and that tour could be the one that claimed him."

Adam reached for the chair, his feet encumbered by his own weight. He sank into the seat, emotionally exposed, his chest cinching tight around his heart.

A tear shined on her cheek. "What if this was the last item you would ever receive from him? He worried what you might remember of him. If somehow he could infuse everything that he was or that he hoped you could be into the one gift he knew you would carry with you every day long after he was gone."

He couldn't respond. She sounded far away, her voice traveled light years to reach him to tell this story. Afraid to breathe lest he dispel the dream, he sat motionless, rooted, and drank in every word.

"Leather," she continued. "The wallet had to be leather. Leather could last you forever if you took care of it. Every boy needs a leather wallet. It can be used for suit-n-tie occasions as well as rough-n-tumble school days. Bi-fold would fit your lifestyle better than a tri-fold. 'It's slimmer in your pocket, and you didn't have all the credit cards that an adult has,' he thought. And black is too serious for a young man. It has to be brown. So your father finally settled on this one. And he held on to it tight, all the way to the register, praying he made the right choice. He soldiered forward, because if this was the very last gift you ever received from him, he wanted to believe it was the best choice, the only choice a strong soldier could give his only son."

Silence strangled his throat, choking words from his mind. *Could this really be true? Did his dad really take that much time sweating over this wallet?* Guilt blanketed over him. He showed appreciation, sure, but not to the magnitude that such a gift deserved. And what if his father hadn't come home?

December returned his wallet, recovered her bear, and sat behind the desk, where Trencher had been. "I envy you so much," she whispered. "Your dad loves you beyond measure. Your wallet tells that story. My dad never came close to loving me."

"The twenty pinned to your sweater," he said, remembering what she told them earlier that day.

She nodded. "Some objects have stronger stories, more emotions behind them, but everything talks to me in some degree. My mom stole that sweater from a second-hand store because she was afraid someone would notice I was cold, not because she wanted me to be warm. The twenty came from the bank on the wrong side of town, a place my dad wasn't supposed to be. And the safety-pin," she pointed to the repair on her bear's bottom, "refuses to shut the fuck up."

"So," Adam cleared his throat when the silence became uncomfortable. "What was it then, um, that you said to Officer Trencher? I watched him leave. I thought he'd seen a ghost."

"Oh, that's right. I didn't tell you yet, did I?"

He thought back. "No, I don't think so."

"That smug son-of-a-jack-o-lantern is my father."

CHAPTER THIRTEEN

Tuesday, 6:00 p.m.

"Y OUR FATHER?" Recoil of her announcement manifested into a sharp pain behind his left eye.

"He doesn't believe he is. I suppose there's a chance he isn't, since my mother was a pathological liar. But there's no denying that he was where he shouldn't have been when he stopped to get money for my mom. He just wanted it all – *me* – to go away."

"I take it your mother never told your Aunt Jean."

"I don't know. I don't think so though. I think Aunt Jeanie hates Officer Trencher regardless. He ran over her dog long before I was born and she never forgave him for it."

"What are you going to do?"

"About what? Officer Trencher? Nothing."

"But," Adam tried finding words through his headache. "He's partially responsible for abandoning you and he's a cop!"

"Look, statute of limitations being what they are, all it would do now is ruin his career. Young and stupid happens to everyone, you know. Sometimes things just are what they are." Pity dampened the glow of her skin, or perhaps it was regret. Her leg jackhammered the floor and Teddy was in burp-position again. The offensive safety-pin shouted *Kiss My Ass* in Gaelic. "How do I tell them how I know, anyway? Everyone already knows I'm nuts. I'll end up in the padded ward at General. I've been there, done that, lost the t-shirt. Their tapioca pudding is disgusting."

Darkness plagued the sky beyond the windows. Adam's head echoed with shrieks of *Demon From Hell*. He tried to remember if he actually took the acetaminophen earlier. The day had been so long, so exhausting, and Hagatha's death only complicated things.

Something bumped Adam's ankle. Sauerkraut looked at him, her ginger fur matted and patchy. He reached down to scratch her ears, but she hissed and ran out the door. "I'll grow on you yet, cat. Just you wait."

"Maybe she'll bring you half a dead mouse, or a small rhinoceros as a present."

"I think she believes I'm supposed to bring her the small rhinoceros. As tribute."

"Or maybe she wants you to find what happened to the tuna casserole."

"Shit, I hope not. Last thing I need is for her to hold a grudge against me for disposing of that crap."

A commotion erupted downstairs. Shrieks bansheed through the old Victorian. Footfalls pounded up the staircase in running strides. Chase popped his head in the doorway and was about to say something when Tess shoved him out of the way. "You two need to get downstairs quick," she coughed. "Hagatha's not dead."

Adam shook his head, trying to wake up. This had to be a nightmare. "Wait, what?"

"No-shit. The-bitch-just-slapped-the-crap-out-of-the-coroner."

"She nailed Chance to a wall with a screw-gun and she's threatening to do the same to Cinnamon. Uncle Todd's trying to fend her off with that blasted fireplace poker, and half the family's on the quest for Grandpa's shotgun." Tess dragged Chase into the room and closed the door on the screams.

Adam slammed his fist into the desk. "I knew it was too good to be true. Damn it!"

"The devil must've thought Mr. Kittridge's stinkin' sister wasn't worth the demon. What do we do now?" December asked. They exchanged glances, hope diminishing from their world. Adam's stomach muscles clenched and he tasted bile in his throat. For a few glorious moments, the family was happy, free.

And now there was nothing to keep Hagatha from retaliating.

"I-have-to-save-my-brother."

December squished her nose and sneered. "I hate spiders."

"I-know, but-he's-still-my-brother."

"Well, I guess we're off the hook for murder now." Adam drummed his fingers absently against the wooden desktop. "Did anyone call the cops? They could send the riot squad."

"Your mom called 'em. I don't know if it'll do any good. Pine Valley doesn't have a riot squad. If Eileen can't calm Hagatha down, no one can."

Adam looked to Tess. "Do we have a plan?"

She shook her head, shrugged, and shook her head again. "I'm way too sober for this shit."

Chase moved to peek out the door, tugging his pants up. Angry screams echoed once again in the parlor. Something had to be done. The woman was out of control. "Wish-we-had-a-poison-dart-gun-or-sumpin.I-might-could-hit-her-from-here."

"Or tomatoes," December suggested. "We could rain ketchup hell down on her from the landing."

"I think that'd only piss her off."

"Adam, I think it's pretty safe to assume she's already pissed." Tess paced, as if a wild mare in a tight corral, testing the strength of a fence. "But we have no tomatoes and that idea, although brilliant, is completely moot."

Adam looked through the ceiling, appealing to heaven for inspiration. "If we had a distraction," he spoke as slow as the idea formed, "if we had a distraction, maybe one of us could sneak up behind her and give her another whack with a candlestick."

"She'll see us the second we come down the staircase," Tess paused on her return stride.

Remembering he helped his father install fire ladders the summer he turned sixteen, Adam pointed to the window. "What about the emergency ladder? We can slip out that way."

"Good idea." Tess opened the window and kicked out the screen. "I wanna be the one to hit her. I owe that bitch. Who's gonna distract Hagatha?"

Adam turned to Chase and held out a fist. "Wanna Roshambo for it?"

"I'll do it," December rose from her seat with her bear cradled under her arm. "You both should go with Tess in case the whole poking-the-whale thing doesn't work."

"You sure?" Adam asked.

"Duh, I wouldn't've offered otherwise."

Tess extended the fire ladder and slipped across the sill. "You coming?"

Chase cinched his pants to his waist. "Let's-do-this."

Adam waited until Chase's head disappeared from the window, "Hey December, in case I don't get the opportunity to later, or in case I forget altogether, I want you to know I'm grateful for my wallet." *That sounded better in my head.*

Her eyes sparkled, two flawless sapphires, and she leaned in to kiss him. "I know."

"Adam! You comin'?" Tess's voice drifted through the open window

Another quick kiss and December slipped out the door. "Yeah, wait up!" Adam hollered down before sliding down the ladder. When his feet hit solid ground, he knew he was as prepared as he was going to be. He kept pace with his cousins and bolted towards the back door, triggering the motion sensor sconces to flood the porch with light. However improvised their plan, they were committed to seeing it through. With any luck, Hagatha's reign of terror would come to a quick conclusion.

CHAPTER FOURTEEN

Tuesday, 6:30 p.m.

THE BACK DOOR SQUEAKED. They stared at each other, afraid to open the door further. No one wanted to give away their element of surprise. They couldn't be sure that the door wouldn't draw attention. Tess groaned. "You know what this means, don't you?"

Adam shrugged, "Wackadoo?"

"Wackadoo." She ran her fingers through her hair. "Son-of-a-shitless-wonder, I hate it when December's smart."

She cleared her throat and spit on the middle hinge. The door hinge drank three rounds of spittle before they could open the door with ease.

"Do not tell her I did that, either one of you," Tess threatened. "I'll never hear the end of it if she finds out. I still get the demented rambling of that stupid poem Billy Banes wrote about me years ago."

Adam did a double-take. Suddenly, his red-head seemed a little less crazy. "You mean that 'Tess I've less to confess' bit December recited this morning was from Burping Billy Banes?"

"Yeah." Tess looked uncomfortable.

"Why-did-Billy-B-write-you-a-poem?"

It was the first time Adam ever saw Tess blush. Scarlet painted her cheeks in vivid hues. "Can we just go get this over with?" she hissed, shoving Chase through the doorway.

They tiptoed through the kitchen and slipped into the dining room. Tess selected a candlestick from the china hutch, bouncing it in her hand as if to test homicidal power. She nodded, satisfied, and peered into the living room.

Adam followed suit, taking up the other side of the doorway. Hagatha's back-end blocked his view of most of the room but it didn't dampen her caterwauling. "All of you, you shouldn't be here anymore. My invalid brother meant nothing to any of you."

"Stop being so damned ugly, Agatha!" It sounded like Mike. And it sounded like he was hiding behind a sofa.

"Ugly? Ugly! I'll show you who's ugly! The whole lazy good-for-nothing bunch of you, that's who. You're all here to steal my money. You're all here to rob me and Eileen blind. Well, I'm on to everyone here, you ungrateful...Stop your bawling, Dahlia. It's not my fault you married a loser and raised a lezbean!"

"Chansh! Chansh! Hang in there, shweetie!"

"And you, Sissy, you drunken whore! Where's that other bastard son of yours? Eh? The one with marbles in his gaping pie-hole?"

Adam pushed Chase back to keep him from charging the room. "Not yet," he mouthed as he signaled to December they were in place.

The red-headed bear-toter leaned over the railing. "Hey Bitch!" She whistled a shrill tone through her fingers. "Ellery Stickney isn't dead. He just didn't come home to YOU!"

The purple tent stopped shrieking and a collective gasp crested from her cornered victims. Candlestick at the ready, Tess darted in behind Hagatha.

Hagatha, however, passed out cold.

"Damn it! I was looking forward to clocking her good." Tess tossed the candlestick aside and it rolled into the hallway.

Taking the opportunity, Sissy ran, narrowly missing the candlestick. "Chansh! Chansh, baby, I'sh comin' to get you!"

Chase hiked his pants up and propelled after his mother. Petal paused before following, "Hippocratic Oath, be damned. Stick a pillow over her nose for all I care."

December danced down the stairs and shimmied through the Kittridge clan of relations. "Does that mean we're not calling 9-1-1?"

Tess narrowed her eyes. "Why are you asking it like that?"

"Well, if we don't call, we'll have to deal with..." she circled her hands above the unmoving Hagatha, emphasizing her words, "all of her."

Tess threw her head back and groaned, "God, I hate it when you're right."

Curtis limped over, nursing a split lip. "It's okay, honey, I've already called them."

"Dad! Shit, what – did Hagatha do that?" Horror flashed across her face. She kicked Hagatha with each word. "You. Miserable. Fucking. Hag!"

Adam grabbed his cousin around the waist and dragged her away from Hagatha's unmoving form. "Let it go, Tess."

"Adam, you spineless wonder...Oh shit I've just turned into that miserable cow. I'm sorry." She hugged him tight. "I'm so sorry."

He squeezed her back, releasing a breath "It's okay Tess, I know you didn't mean it the way she'd have meant it."

Chase tripped over his pants as he returned to the living room. "We-pried-Chance-loose-from-the-wall.Petal's-quick-too.She's-already-given-him-stitches."

Chance's swagger was more pronounced. He clutched a red-stained bandage to his forearm and he grinned like a Cheshire cat. "Petal let me have the good drugs."

Adam released Tess and looked towards the hallway. "What'd you do with Sissy and Petal? They get lost down there?"

"Ma-passed-out-at-the-sight-of-the-blood," Chase pointed down the hallway. "She's-sleeping-it-off-in-that-spare-bedroom. Petal's-looking-after-her."

"We oughta give Petal a medal," Tess's giggle over-flowed through her fingers. "And now I'm rhyming like December."

December hugged her bear. "See Teddy, I told you Tess liked us."

"I wouldn't go that far, Wackadoo," Tess responded, still laughing. "You're just contagious."

December squished her nose. "Close enough for government work."

Curtis tugged on his daughter's sleeve. "Your mom and I are taking off. She can't take any more of this tonight. You comin'?"

"Adam'll give me a ride."

He glanced up when his name was volunteered, "I'm not leaving until tomorrow, Tess."

"That's fine."

Curtis nodded. "Then come say goodbye to your mother."

The evening was cool and the family retreated to the expanse of front porch and lawn, shedding the horrible stuffiness of the house.

Bats worked silently above them, clearing the air of pesky mosquitoes, and in the distance, the screech of an owl echoed through the valley. Adam sucked in fresh air and popped tension from his neck. The breeze felt like freedom.

Tess nudged his ribs. "Mom, Adam has something to ask us."

Adam froze while Dahlia and Curtis looked expectant. "I, uh, well...It can wait."

Tess didn't let him off the hook that easy. "He wants to turn Grandpa's house into a bed and breakfast."

"Like I said, it can wait," Adam said, stepping on Tess's foot. "Let's get beyond the train wreck lying on the floor in there before we make any plans for anything."

December shook her head. "It's not a train wreck as much as a beached whale."

It was the first real smile Adam had seen grace Dahlia's face all day. "Miss Ashby, as rude as that may sound, I believe you are correct. And Adam," Dahlia cast her weary eyes towards the house, "I see no reason why this place couldn't be a bed and breakfast. Let's get together and come up with a business plan."

Tess sighed. "I'll be damned all to Hell, Mom. I never thought you'd agree to that."

"With the right business plan, it's a smart move. And I dislike that the house is in such a state of disrepair. It would be nice to see it useful once again, don't you think?"

CHAPTER FIFTEEN

Tuesday, 7:15 p.m.

SINCE THE THREAT OF A MURDER CHARGE WAS GONE, and since the will was read, the family began to split apart. Goodbyes were tearful and exhausted, but exchanged with a promise to get together again soon. Cars jockeyed for position out of the driveway, avoiding the approaching ambulance. A few brave souls offered to stick around and at least help with the dishes, but Adam's mother insisted they depart. "Traffic out of town shouldn't be a problem, but once you get to the highway, that's a different matter altogether," she said.

No one argued the point, but Adam knew it wasn't out of a desire to shirk responsibility. Dealings with Hagatha induced emotional stress, and the general sentiment was that it had been a very long day indeed.

Adam counted who was left, comparing the number to the bedrooms available. Todd said he wasn't leaving until he finished his whiskey, and Cinnamon remained at his side. They'd probably take Todd's old room. Petal, who still hadn't emerged from the hallway, could take Dahlia's old bedroom. And Sissy couldn't drive, not in her condition, and should stay in the spare room where she passed out.

That left his mother, who of course would have her old room. And the cousins...

Adam couldn't imagine anyone taking the master that night, not with Grandpa Lum's personal affects still haunting the room. As Tess and the twins led the EMTs in to check on Hagatha, Adam worked out the sleeping logistics in the living room. Tess could have the couch; the twins could fight over the armchair. Then he could fetch the cots from the cellar storage. They should be fine camping out unless Sauerkraut decided to wage war in the middle of the night.

Maybe he should have saved the tuna barge.

December showed no signs of wanting to leave. Adam hoped it had something to do with him, although he got the feeling she just liked being around chaos. They lingered together on the porch, leaving the emergency crew to work in the living room. Moving Hagatha was a challenge Adam didn't want to witness. "So, you sticking around?" he asked, searching for a topic.

The red-head nodded, her bear locked upside-down against her chest behind folded arms. "This is way more funner than Aunt Jeanie's."

"We're a little short on beds I think, but you're welcome to crash here anyway."

She cocked her head, her face pinched and suspicious. "Are you asking me to sleep with you?"

"No," he felt flames burn his cheeks. "Please, not with my mom in the house. That'd be too...weird."

"You mean you've never smuggled a girl in your room when you were in high school?" She smirked. His cheeks burned hotter. "Not once?"

"Um, I plead the Fifth."

"You did!"

"Maybe. Once."

She raised an eyebrow.

He scratched the base of his neck. "Twice," he lied. He wanted to put his head in the freezer. Heat built up on the covered porch like it was prepping for an inferno. He coughed and tucked his hands in his pockets.

Her sapphire eyes sparkled in the light filtering through the window. They said she didn't believe him. He didn't care. He stole another kiss.

"Agatha, stay put!"

His mother's warning tumbled out the door, dispelling the heat and sending ice through his veins. Adam entered the living room in three strides, and December collided with his back when he stopped short. Hagatha teetered on her feet, waving Tess's candlestick in wild circles, keeping the EMTs at bay.

"Agatha, don't drop the candlestick." Tess blurred by, reaching for the fireplace poker. "I've been waiting to beat the shit out of you all night."

"Tess, you're not helping."

"Get out of my way Aunt Eily," Tess wielded her rod of fury like an angry god. "It'll be my pleasure to go to jail for murdering this bitch."

"Tess, Agatha. Both of you, STOP!" Adam closed his eyes against the inevitable. His mother was about to jump in the middle of it all.

Cha-chink.

Adam's eyes opened at the unmistakable sound. Todd stood at the top of the stairs with a shotgun pointed at the back of Agatha's head. "I can reach out and touch her from here," he said. "That means I win."

Agatha spun about and the candlestick fell to the ground with a thud. "Todd, you ass–"

"Try me, Agatha. Right now, your only option is to get on that damn stretcher and let the EMTs do their FUCKING jobs. The next words outta your fucking mouth better be *Yes Todd*. Do you understand me?"

Hagatha raised a fist and took a step forward. Her foot landed on the candlestick and her two large arms flew up in the air and circled for purchase that never came. She screamed the entire fall to the floor. The crash sent a mini-quake through the old house, dislodging pictures from the walls and rattling the crystal and china in the cabinet.

"Crap," Oscar Lindsay groaned. "I was hoping we wouldn't have to lift her."

"I heard she beat the crap out of the coroner. Is he okay?" Adam asked.

"Yeah, he checked himself into County General not long ago. Prognosis is good and his bones should heal." Oscar scratched his head and looked to his coworkers. "How do you want to approach this, boys?"

"I am not a useless cripple!" Hagatha shrieked. She rolled from her back and onto her hands and knees with the speed and effort of an upturned turtle. "Well, don't just stand there. Help me!"

Sauerkraut, in her infinite cat-wisdom, sauntered in the room behind Hagatha hissing, tail fully fluffed. No one moved.

"I said help me. God, what do my taxes pay for anyway?" Hagatha flailed an arm, attempting to use the couch for a hand up.

Sauerkraut stood up on her hind legs and launched. All four paws and a jaw full of pointy teeth sank into Hagatha's backside.

She screamed again and jolted up to her feet, smacking as best she could towards the cat she couldn't quite reach.

"I really need to start carrying a camera," December said. "Or one of those smart phones. We could've made a fortune on the internet several times over already."

They watched the train wreck wiggle and writhe while cries of "Demon from HELL" flooded the night. It was a pitiable scene, but no one seemed to be in the mood for pity. It felt victorious, watching Hagatha spin and curse and spin. Even Adam's mother seemed delighted at the raucous, bright-eyed and glowing. Adam turned to December and grinned. "Want some popcorn?"

CHAPTER SIXTEEN

Tuesday, 8:30 p.m.

"I CAN'T BELIEVE SHE ACTUALLY WENT IN THE AMBULANCE," Adam's mother dunked a platter into the soapy water in the sink and sponged some crusted cheese from its surface.

Todd swirled his drink, ice cubes clanking against the sides of the glass. "Well, as pig-headed as that woman is, she still knows not to argue with the business end of a shotgun."

Adam leaned against the kitchen island, spooned some ice-cream, and winced at the shock of cold against his back teeth. "What gets me is that Oscar insisted they couldn't find a pulse. How was Hagatha even standing?"

December stole a bite from Adam's ice-cream and cast him a sly look from the corner of her eyes. "Zombie?"

Adam shook his head. "Zombies can't move that fast."

December laughed and offered to take up the drying. "It'll go faster that way, Mrs. Bingham."

"All right, towel's right there." Eileen gestured towards the blue fluff on the sideboard. "Be careful with this platter. I'm not sure exactly how old it is but it came through the civil war."

December nodded and took careful possession of the antique with dishtowel draped hands. Adam watched her turn the piece over and wipe and over and wipe while his mother selected a plate from the pile of dirty dishes next to her. "Sauerkraut doesn't like many people," Adam said between spoonfuls, "but she seems to really have it in for Hagatha."

"We should probably discuss what we're going to do with that old mouser." Todd sipped his drink. "I imagine her quality of life is going to go down the shitter from here on out."

The ice-cream pooled into soup, and Adam contemplated discarding his spoon and drinking from the bowl. "Ah, leave her be, Uncle Todd. Grandpa hasn't fed her in forever, so she's earning her keep catching wild things, yeah? So she's mangy-looking and unpredictable. If Hagatha thinks she's a demon from hell, don't you think it's worth keeping around?"

Todd pointed with his glass, "You make a fair case. Why didn't you want to be a lawyer?"

"You keep way too many hours for me. I'm basically a lazy slob." Adam slurped the last of the ice-cream soup from his bowl.

"That's a fair point, too." Todd raised his glass in toast formation. "The prosecution moves to dismiss all charges."

December placed the platter aside and accepted the plate from Adam's mother in the same careful manner. She ran the drying rag in tiny circles. "Adam's not lazy. He's going to start a bed-and-breakfast."

Todd frowned and Eileen turned around. "He's *what?*" Eileen asked. "You're what?"

Damn it, December. Adam cringed and fought to find words, feeling the room shrink around him. "I, uh, we haven't discussed it yet. It was just an idea."

Todd brought a finger to his chin. "The location for your bed and breakfast would be, where, exactly?"

December tossed a wink over her shoulder. "Where else? Here, in Mr. Kittridge's house."

Adam couldn't read his mother's expression. "You want to open Dad's house up for strangers, Adam?"

"Well, not for free or anything like that Ma."

She turned enough to drop her sponge in the sink. "Dad didn't leave our house to you; he left it to my sister and me."

"I know, Ma," Adam ran a frustrated hand through his hair, half-wishing Hagatha was back. At least, that way the focus would be elsewhere. "Like I said, we haven't discussed it yet and it was just an idea anyway."

Todd shrugged, "Eily, I like it. It's a great idea."

She had that worried look, the one she'd give Adam when he climbed a too-tall tree. "Mom, remember we talked about it more than once? Give us solid ground, a place to grow roots. Dad's gotta retire from service someday. He'll need a place to go."

"I know we talked about it, Adam, but Dahlia..."

"Like I said. We haven't had a chance to discuss it. I'm not making plans. I'm just dreaming."

Todd shrugged, "Say what you want to, Adam, but you get your mom and Dahlia on board, I won't charge for any legal advice or filings you need done on behalf of the bed and breakfast."

"Really?"

"Just think. You'll have the weight of my entire firm behind you. At any time."

Adam looked to his mother. A spark of light danced in her weary eyes. He could tell that with Todd's support, she was tempted. She sighed. "We'll talk."

Tess poked her head into the kitchen, "Do you know that Chance has brass balls?"

December looked confused. "Where does he keep them?"

Adam laughed, grateful for the distraction. "Why do you say that, Tess?"

"Because he had the nerve to ask Petal to give him a medical marijuana card now that he's handicapped."

"Figures. What did Petal do?"

"She pinched his ear until he rescinded his request."

"Yup, that's Petal."

Eileen submerged the tuna casserole dish in the sink. "I'm surprised this thing is empty. I didn't see anyone eat it."

Todd moved so Tess could open the fridge. "That's 'cause no one did," she said, her voice muffled from speaking into the icebox. "Except the pigs. Adam had the sense to dispose of the glop at the pig-pen earlier."

"That was a smart idea. Sauerkraut didn't even have any of it. She just scratched, belly deep in the stuff like it was a litter box." Eileen scrubbed at the stubborn cheesy edges, cursing. "I think Agatha put cement in the cheese."

"I don't understand why you're trying to clean it for that fat bitch," Tess said, closing the fridge door, cold beer in hand.

"Tessie Glynne, please, there really isn't any need for name-calling."

"Aunt Eily, Hagatha's a nasty person."

"And you're an angry one." Eileen added more soap to the rim. "She can change, and so can you."

Tess frowned. "I'm not angry, I'm just mad as Hell."

Adam saw his mother's shoulders shake in quiet laughter. She pushed her hair back with the dry part of her forearm. "Well, I guess I stand corrected. The point is I don't like name-calling; no matter how justified it may or may not be. And I'd appreciate it if you didn't resort to that within my earshot."

Tess used the heavy sigh that Adam knew was born of sarcasm. "Adam, how good's her hearing?"

He shook his head. "She can hear the whisper of a bat's fart ten leagues away."

"Oh, enough you two." His mom's shoulders danced as she paused in the scrubbing. "Look, it doesn't cost much to do a simple act of kindness, even for someone difficult to get along with."

The dish slipped between her fingers as Eileen tried to pass it along. December reacted, scooping up the casserole before it hit the floor. As quickly as she fetched it up, however, she dropped it on the counter. Her freckles paled as a look of horror crossed her face. "The pigs!"

She catapulted by Todd and through the door into the night. Tess set her beer down and tugged at Adam's sleeve. "Come on. Time to go after Wackadoo."

Adam paused to fetch the flashlight from the junk drawer as he followed, hoping there was enough juice left in the batteries for a blitzkrieg run to the sty.

CHAPTER SEVENTEEN

Tuesday, 9:00 p.m.

"DECEMBER!" Adam hated running. He hated uneven ground. He hated running over uneven ground. He wasn't wearing the appropriate shoes, for one thing. For another thing, he hated running.

Pain shot through his shins as his long legs propelled him out of a gopher crater big enough to swallow a house. Adam thought of high school every time he had to run. First, the bullies chased him until his growth spurt. Then his physical education teachers tricked him onto the track team. He was their star athlete, and he hated every moment of it.

"Adam!" Tess's voice trailed after him. "I can't see in the dark you know!"

Well, he hated running anyway. He paused long enough for his cousin to catch up and then jogged alongside her, sweeping the flashlight back and forth before them so they could better anticipate pitfalls. "December's either got the eyes of an owl or the ears of a bat. It is pitch black out here," Adam said between breaths, concentrating on the vegetation and earth the weak amber glow revealed.

"Not to mention...she's lightning fast." Tess sputtered and gasped. "What's she worried...about the pigs for? They've...got a sty...they go into...every night."

"I haven't a clue, Tess."

"Well, she's...your girlfriend."

"She's not."

"I know you, Adam...You two are sucking face...She's your girlfriend."

"Tess, just stop...What the fu..."

December knelt in the pigpen below the sty's floodlight. The Hereford sows lay at her knees, unmoving. Light danced in fresh tears on December's cheeks. "Mr. Kittridge's stinkin' sister killed them," she cried.

Tess crashed into the fence. "Who? Hagatha? She killed the pigs? On purpose?"

"Well, no, she meant to kill everyone else, only Adam fed her tuna casserole to the pigs."

Adam's thoughts reached critical mass and exploded inside his skull as he tried to make sense of the statement. That the pigs were dead, that truth was undeniable. He could see them, dead, their eyes hollow and sad. And December's tears tugged at his heartstrings.

But Hagatha. A killer?

Tess launched over the fence and poked a finger at the nearest pig. "It's not breathing."

"Duh. Dead things generally don't breathe Tess."

"December, what, how?"

"That fucking bitch put arsenic in the casserole." December stroked a pig's ears. "Sauerkraut saved our lives."

Adam found some words, discarded them for others, and at the end, settled for a stuttered sigh. "I don't..."

"I'm going to kill her." December wiped her eyes against her sleeve. "Don't worry. I promise I'll make it slow and painful."

"As tempting as that sounds," Tess scratched her head while a frown developed above her chin, "do we know for certain that Hagatha intentionally tried to kill us all?"

December snorted. "What, you don't think she's capable?"

Tess looked affronted. "Well, she's a miserable bitch but..."

"Well, you'd better start believing it. She's killed before."

Verbal paralysis affected Adam a second time as his brain fumbled to catch up. Tess was quicker. "Pigs or people."

The ground crunched in footfalls beyond the circle of light. Adam turned. His mother and Todd emerged from the shadows. They both looked confused. "You're saying Aunt Agatha did that to those pigs?" Todd pointed. "Through the casserole?"

"That's not all. That miserable cow killed Mr. Kittridge," December delivered the accusation without flinching.

No one had a voice. Adam focused on the pigs and imagined what reality was really like. There had to be people in that alternate universe, good descent people who did good descent things. Surely there was a world without Hagatha.

Todd leaned up against the fence, an angry hunger scoring his face. "December Ashby, this is the second accusation I've heard from you today besmirching someone's character."

"This one is no less true than the other. Mr. Kittridge's stinkin' sister wanted to kill everyone in that house today, just like she killed her brother."

"Wait," Eileen looked between them, like an arcade ball between paddles and kickers, before bringing her confused stare to full bore at December. "Aunt Agatha killed Dad? How long have you known? Why are you just telling us this now?"

December rose. Mud coated her shoes and jeans where they had contacted the earth. "Mrs. Bingham, I only suspicioned that Mr. Kittridge died at her hands. The pigs just confirmed it."

She touched the casserole dish in the kitchen, Adam remembered, fighting the bile rising in his throat.

"We don't have proof." Todd's lawyer voice leaked out, delivering an eerie reason to the circus of emotions. "The casserole dish has been washed."

Tess shifted her weight. Adam felt the hatred pulsing from her in waves. He'd never seen her so angry she couldn't stand still, like butter in a hot skillet. "Hagatha needs to die!"

No one, not even Adam's mother, objected. December raised her hand, volunteering. "I said earlier, I'll do it," she said.

Todd covered his ears and shut his eyes tight. "I'm not listening."

Tess shook her head, a violent negative. "The Hell you will! I owe that bitch! It's my fucking turn to whack her with a fireplace poker!"

December met Adam's gaze, her eyes sparkling in the floodlight. "Tess, you're whole family has lost way too much already. It makes more sense for me to do it. I've nothing to lose and I have a history of mental illness, right? I'll take care of her. It will be painful and slow. I'll even video it if you want me to."

Has the world gone completely nuts? Adam ran a frustrated hand through his hair, thinking with clarity for the first time since he arrived at the pigs' slaughterhouse. "Look, far be it for me to be the voice of reason here. I mean, I've talked about murdering her all day. And I truly doubt that a jury would convict anyone if they were caught. But let's take a second and think this through."

"What's there to think about?" Tess spit. "December's trying to steal my righteous kill."

"No, that's not what I'm getting at Tess." Adam pulled Todd's hands away from his ears. "We've already got enough to convict her of other crimes today. Several counts of assault with a deadly weapon, kidnapping, and what's that one about placing an emergency call when there's no emergency? And I don't recall anyone actually inviting Hagatha to the wake, so trespassing and harassment could stick too, if we're clever."

Eileen folded her arms around herself. "Chance and Petal could file charges, certainly. And the coroner. That would force Officer Trencher to arrest her in her hospital room."

Todd tapped a finger at his chin. "You know, we could still get her on murder. We know for a fact Agatha brings the tuna casserole every year. The tuna always gets fed to the pigs. This year the pigs have died. We have a necropsy done on the pigs, and those results will give us the suspicious circumstance to convince a medical examiner to do an autopsy on Dad. When we know the poison, law enforcement can get a search warrant to check Agatha's house where they can find enough evidence to arrest her on suspicion of murder."

Tess groaned, long and high-pitched. "Does nobody here understand that I don't give a shit about justice? I want whack Hagatha like a piñata!"

Adam's mother surprised them all. "Oh, Tessie Glynne, get off your high-horse. You're at the end of a very long line of people that are entitled to hit that piñata. You don't get to take cuts before me."

CHAPTER EIGHTEEN

Tuesday, 10:00 p.m.

"ANYONE HOME?" A familiar voice drifted through to the kitchen just as Adam returned from the sty with his family.

"Archie!" Eileen rushed to the living room.

Adam followed in time to see his mom leap into his dad's arms in a tender exchange of kisses and hugs. "I got here as soon as I could," his dad whispered.

"I wasn't expecting you at all." Eileen wiped fresh tears from her eyes. "So much has happened...I don't even know where to begin."

"I've only a couple days leave, and that's only because I was allowed to catch the jump-seat on a supply plane. I'm hoping I won't miss the funeral?"

December slipped her hand into Adam's, sidetracking him from his parents' reunion. "You're really, really lucky, you know that?" she said.

Adam thought about it for a moment. He spent most of his young adult life drifting through his days, spinning about like a weather vane whenever the wind changed. He lost himself somewhere along the way, focusing on meaningless relationships and forgetting the strength of his roots. His family was the anchor he'd been missing.

And it took a crazy redhead to remind him where he should be. In one day, December managed to both ground him and send his spirit soaring. He squeezed her hand. "I think I'm starting to."

"Good," December said, pulling away. "Now that that is settled, I'm going to find Teddy."

Adam chuckled and let her go, aware that his parents were both staring at him. "Hi Dad, you have no idea how glad I am to see you."

His dad crossed the room. He was a tall man too, with a stature of a demi-god. His father offered up his usual bro-hug, more of a handshake with a bump to the shoulders, but Adam was overwhelmed. He swallowed the lump in his throat and gave his father a solid hug.

His father coughed, pulling back. "Hey, what's this all about?"

"Oh, nothing much. I'm a crap son, Dad." Adam tucked his hands in his pockets and stared at his feet. "You deserve better than what you got."

His dad's face was cast in steel and his voice gruff. "Say that again and I'll send you out to the woodshed. I couldn't be prouder of you."

"Yeah, well, I never thanked you for my wallet." Adam rocked on his heels. "And I should have."

"Uh, well, you're welcome." His face softened. The moment lingered until Todd appeared in the doorway. "Todd, it's good to see you. How's Fancy, er, no, it was Ariel wasn't it?"

Todd laughed. "Ariel overstayed her welcome two months ago, so I've no idea how she is."

"Should've known. And Tess. Did your folks already head back?"

Tess nodded. "Yeah, Hagatha took a lot out of everybody today, Uncle Archie."

Adam saw his dad shiver and grimace. "Eily told me Aunt Agatha went to the hospital. She gonna be okay?"

Tess snorted. "Not if I can help it."

December wiggled her finger at Adam from the hallway. He excused himself, letting the others get his dad up to speed, and followed her down to the cellar. "What's up?"

"I found something down here. I thought you should see it." The light complained in crackling hisses as the switch flipped it awake. They descended down the staircase for the third time that day and crossed the concrete floor.

"So we're not coming down here to make out?" He was only half-joking.

She squished her nose at him, "Maybe later. You need to see this first."

Some of the pot-bear piles had been redistributed to expose the corner. A large wooden sign leaned against the north wall. Adam helped December brush a layer of dust from the facade. Kittridge Valley Bed And Breakfast materialized in the same blue paint that matched the exterior of the house.

"Wait," Adam said, rubbing the base of his neck. "I don't get it. Is this a souvenir? Did Grandpa Lum get this from somewhere?"

December smiled. "Yes, Mr. Kittridge got this from somewhere, but he ordered it specifically, just after your grandmother passed away. He got it for your mom and her sister, Mrs. Archer."

"He knew?" Adam's heart skipped a beat. "Grandpa knew we wanted a bed and breakfast?"

She nodded, tracing the letters as if she painted it herself. "He wanted to see this place live again. With your grandmother gone, the sunshine left too. And his stinkin' sister kept him so bereft of joy, he let the place fall into disrepair. But what he wanted for you, for your mom, for your family, was to breathe happiness back into this house."

"You're amazing, you know that?"

Her hand dropped to her side. "No, I'm not."

"Yes, yes you are. You find beauty in the simplest of things, in the best of people. That's an amazing gift. It makes you special."

Her eyes watered when she turned to look at him. "I've got issues. I'm not perfect, remember? How does that make me special?"

"Oh, take a compliment, will you? I'm bad at them. I don't notice stuff. Like Tess. She's probably changed her hairstyle a gazillion times but I don't catch on until a week after I've seen her."

"Is that why you don't know?"

Crap. Come on, think! "You mean, about earlier? The secret you refused to tell me?"

She chewed on her lower lip. "It's not my secret to tell, actually, but Tess...can you keep a secret?"

"Probably not."

"No, I mean it. It's something you should know. The adults know. We assumed the twins didn't because they're potheads."

"But you're saying everyone else knows?"

"Yeah. So can you keep a secret?"

He sucked in a deep breath and coughed out a layer of dust. "Sure, fire away."

"Tess is adopted."

"Oh that, okay." Adam remembered when his parents explained how Uncle Curtis and Aunt Dahlia had a three year old child. When he was five, he thought some kids were born that old, like they came out of the oven well done. "I knew that."

"Oh? Did you know she's had a crush on you for forever?"

"What?" Adam frowned. He was dense but he didn't know he was that dense.

"The reason for the animosity earlier, she was jealous. We thought you understood that."

"Ew, she's my cousin."

December folded her arms and raised an eyebrow. "Yes, she knows that. You don't see her tricking you down into the cellar to make out with you, do you?"

He was dense, but he wasn't that dense. "Sooo, we are going to make out then?"

She squished her nose and stuck out her tongue. "Duh, I didn't drag you down here to get Teddy out of time out. You're pretty fucking thick-headed sometimes."

"Shut up." Adam grabbed her head with both hands and kissed her.

CHAPTER NINETEEN

Wednesday, 8:00 a.m.

THE SUN KISSED ADAM'S BROW as it crested the foothills and streamed through the living room window. He woke from his cot, working stiffness from his joints. With an awkward stagger, he stepped over the twins and made his way to the ground floor bathroom, answering the call of his morning constitutional.

He returned after washing and the others hadn't stirred from their posts. A mountain of blankets hid most of Tess as she slept on the couch. December was curled in a fetal position around her bear in the armchair. The twins were still dead weight on the floor.

Adam heard movement in the kitchen and soon caught the whiff of Grandpa's cowboy coffee. The chicory-infused java would serve to wake the whole house as it had Adam's stomach. He stumbled to the kitchen before he realized his feet responded. His father balanced a couple dozen eggs across his forearm as he prepped a skillet on the stove for breakfast.

"Mornin' Dad," Adam's words tumbled out in a graveled grumble.

"Is that even English?" his father chuckled. "Make yourself useful and grab the milk."

117

"Right." The cold air from the fridge felt amazing. He pulled the grated cheese out as well as the milk, knowing that his father would ask for it next.

"Are you cognizant yet?" His dad started breaking eggs into the buttered skillet.

"Working on it." Adam set the dairy items on the side-board and reached for a coffee mug.

"Good. Your mother and I had a chance to talk last night. Apart from the whole mess with Hagatha, this boarding house idea..."

Adam groaned over the snapping and popping of cooking eggs. "I'm almost sorry I ever brought that up. I should have waited until after the rest of this crap blowed over."

"No, we agree with you, actually. It's a good idea. It'll take some time to get this place up to snuff, but a little elbow grease and some pull with the zoning authority, I think it could work."

Coffee warmed the mug in Adam's hands and steam opened the pores across his nose as he inhaled. "And I thought, there's enough of our family local that we could take turns. You know, take over during vacations and stuff, so none of us get burned out."

"But first," Todd announced from the doorway, "first we have to teach you that cowboy coffee isn't drinkable and shouldn't be served to anyone anywhere."

Adam shrugged. "It's better than that crap you buy from that overpriced cafe in the bookstore."

Cinnamon peeked around Todd's shoulders. "Do I smell food? Didn't we eat enough yesterday, Toddy? Why is your family always eating?"

"Don't worry, Cinnamon Honey," Todd kissed her cheek. "I intend to spirit you away before I force you to eat anything. Speaking of which, we should get going. We have to make a pit stop by the hospital to make sure the medical examiner got the pigs last night."

"Who, Agatha?" she asked.

Todd sighed, "If only we were so lucky."

"Will the pigs be enough to start the investigation into Grandpa's death?" Adam asked over his coffee mug.

"Absolutely," Todd said, squirming as Cinnamon attached her mouth to his earlobe. "Gotta run, boys. Please tell Eily that I'll call her later."

"I can't keep track of his women," Adam's father said as the lovers left through the kitchen door. "And somehow, I'm okay with it. Todd never struck me as the settling down type."

"This is the first one I remember ever liking," Adam agreed. "She may be short a few bricks for a wall, but she's hot and sweet."

"My CO calls that type number six."

"Number six?"

"Yeah, like Chinese takeout, with number six, you get sticky and sweet eggroll. But you're hungry an hour later."

Adam groaned. "That's wrong."

His dad laughed. "Only 'cause it's true."

"Sooo, intentionally changing the subject. If we're going to do the bed-and-breakfast thing. December found a wooden sign in the cellar that Grandpa apparently got for us with the idea that we set one up."

"Hmm, is that why you two were down there for an hour?" His dad turned the cheesy scrambled eggs into a bowl. "You were looking for a sign?"

Were we that obvious? "We found the sign while looking for the cot for sleeping arrangements." Adam coughed. That didn't come out like he wanted to say it. "The point is Grandpa gave us his support."

"That's okay, Son. I like her, too. She's nuts, but she's cute. Just, uh, well..." He cast a furtive glance through to the dining room and dropped his voice to a whisper, "Keep it wrapped, eh?"

"Really, Dad." Adam hated having these conversations with his dad, at least within potential earshot of his potential girlfriend. Over a hunting trip, they were two guys bonding. In Grandpa's house, it only felt awkward.

Sausage, hash-browns and biscuits were pulled from the oven when the timer went off. The silent call to breakfast echoed through the house, and bodies of the almost living materialized in the kitchen for plates of food. December nudged close to Adam at the dining room table, a gesture he took to mean her mind hadn't changed from yesterday. She was still into him.

"Where's Todd and Cinnamon?" Adam's mother glanced about before commandeering a place at the table.

"They took off already. Todd's going to follow up with the medical examiner and bring our suspicions before the district attorney." Adam's father said between mouthfuls.

"So we're actually going to pursue this? Convicting Aunt Agatha of murder?"

"Don't tell me you're getting cold feet Eily," Adam's father gave her a hardened soldier's face. "The woman needs to be brought to justice and you yourself admitted to wanting to take a crack at her last night."

"No, I'm not getting cold feet," she placed her fork down and leaned against the table on an elbow. "It's just...things got so out of hand so fast yesterday. I don't feel like we got to give Dad a proper send off because we had to deal with Agatha all day."

"Mrs. Bingham, there's no reason we can't have another Bon Voyage for Mr. Kittridge." December reached for her glass of orange juice. "That's the best part about celebrating a life isn't it? You can do it as many times as you need to get the job done."

"You're right of course, December, but I still feel a little cheated, I suppose."

December swallowed and wiped her mouth on her sleeve. "Well, Mr. Kittridge's stinkin' sister has a lot to answer for. You know he suspected she took all of Mrs. Kittridge's jewelry, don't you?"

"Dad what?" Eileen moved her elbow and sat up straight.

December nodded. "Yup, it was one of the reasons he was so eager to piss her off by having me take her car on joyrides through town, and why he never wanted her to spend the night. Every time she was left alone in the house, Mr. Kittridge would find another piece of his wife's jewelry missing. And he couldn't keep an eye on her all the time, not with needing to tend the farm and stuff."

"Why did he never say anything?" Adam's mother looked crushed, like an abandoned puppy.

"Mr. Kittridge never wanted to upset anyone. Well, except for his stinkin' sister that is. That, and he was also distrustful of his own memory, especially towards the end. He stopped cooking dinner because he was afraid he'd leave the fire on and burn the house down or something."

"But all those containers in the fridge, the ones that were there before the wake. Where did those leftovers come from?"

December shrugged. "I guess they came from his stinkin' sister. She was visiting here practically every day there at the end."

"We haven't thrown them away, have we?" Adam rose from his seat, ready to raid the trash.

"Well yes, but that's because I didn't know how long any of it had been there and I didn't want anyone getting sick... where are you going?"

"To follow a hunch." Adam said. "Some of those dishes may still have the poison in them."

CHAPTER TWENTY

Wednesday, 2:00 p.m.

ADAM PACED IN THE HALLWAY near Hagatha's room at County General, plotting her demise. He could pull out her breathing tube and brace the door so the nurses couldn't respond to a code blue. Staph infections were sometimes fatal: perhaps he could find a stray culture waiting for destruction and expose Hagatha's wounds to the infection. Or, he could find an empty syringe somewhere and inject an air bubble in her veins.

The empty syringe was the most promising method. It was the least likely to be detected, and a heart attack would be expected in a woman of Hagatha's size.

Resolved, he started for her room, and stopped.

Adam's parents appeared in the hallway. December trailed behind clutching her bear. Perhaps murder with witnesses wasn't one of his better plans. He swallowed a sigh and forced a smile, giving a half-hearted wave their direction.

"Todd should be here soon," Adam's mother said. "What's the word on Agatha's condition?"

Adam pointed towards the nurses' station. "They said she slipped into a coma early this morning. They were pretty excited about it, actually."

"I'll bet." December hugged her bear. "If she's comatose, she's not going anywhere. Wanna get some lunch?"

Adam's father gave an approving wink. "We'll wait here for Todd," he added.

"So why is your family having a reunion at Mr. Kittridge's stinkin' sister's hospital bed?" December asked as Adam escorted her to the elevator.

He pushed the down-arrow button. "Todd's doing something lawyerly as next-of-kin regarding an advanced directive or DNR or whatever for Hagatha. Mom feels the need to be here for her aunt because she's the only person who seems to care for her. Dad's here because Mom's here."

The elevator doors opened and they boarded the carriage. "And why are you here?"

"I was going to kill her until you all showed up."

December pouted. "I'm sorry I showed up then."

"Eh, it's probably for the best." He shrugged. "Maybe."

As the doors opened to the lobby, Adam caught sight of Tess arguing with a security guard at the guest desk. Her pitched voice echoed off the walls, causing passersby to look in askance her direction. Adam groaned as f-bombs dropped and onlookers scurried away.

"Wonder what that's all about?" December craned her neck as a family crossed in front of her.

The security guard fiddled with the snap that attached a pair of handcuffs to his belt. Adam called out in hopes to distract them both and diffuse the situation. "Tess! Let's go get lunch."

He felt the venom of her glare from across the lobby. "Keep the fuck out of this, Adam!"

"She's gonna get herself arrested." Helplessness kept him from springing to action, immobilizing both his feet and his brain.

December touched his shoulder. "I can help, if you want."

"How?"

"Just, just promise me you won't laugh."

"Um..."

"Or get mad. You can't laugh or get mad."

"I promise."

"Pinky swear." She wiggled her little finger in front of his nose.

"God, are we still in high school or something?" Adam sighed, but capitulated, looping his little finger around hers. "I swear. Go save Tess from herself."

"Here," she thrust her bear against his chest with a heavy shove. "Don't let Teddy out of your sight. Meet you in the cafeteria."

December charged through the milling looky-loos, leaping over a toddler, clearing him by at least three feet. The security guard must have heard her coming, for he turned towards her, a slow reaction comprised of too little, too late. December snatched the handcuffs from his hand and bolted down the adjacent corridor.

"Ho...*shit*," Adam breathed.

The security guard seemed trapped in a different dimension. Each delayed movement wasted precious time as his quarry slipped further and further away. When his feet finally engaged in a run, the resulting scene was reminiscent of a Keystone Cop silent motion picture.

Tess laughed. "Run, Puppet! Run!"

The spectacle over, the on-lookers moved on and Adam's long stride made quick work of the lobby floor. "Tess, wha–"

Her turn was military crisp. "Oh, here we go. Adam, please. Don't start with me."

Pain seared his heart. She'd said mean-spirited things to him before, but it never bothered him. Adam always chalked it up to her abrasive attitude, the attitude which he loved most about Tess. But this... Somewhere, a straw obliterated a camel's back.

He retaliated through a clenched jaw. "Well, pardon the shit out of me for giving a flying fuck."

Tears reflected in her eyes as her hand caught her mouth. "Adam, I–"

"Póg mo thóin, Tess." He tucked the bear like a football in the nook of his arm and walked away, feeling sick. Grandpa Lum was the glue that kept the Kittridge clan together, and the horsepower that kept the clan purring like a kitten. His death drove a gaping chasm that fractured his family, and Adam was beginning to believe that it would never be repaired.

Adam was grateful for the clinical ambiance in the cafeteria. He wanted to think, or actually, he wanted not to think. He took up a table in a forgotten corner and did his best to look like a shadow. Propping December's bear up against the napkin dispenser, he sank into the unforgiving plastic chair, ignored the prickle of static electricity that crawled up his back, and waited.

The cafeteria was not designed for lengthy stays. The stark decor and impossible furniture all but screamed *Trespassers Will Be Shot*. Still, several visitors and doctors drifted in and out like transients in shifts before December plopped in the seat opposite him, flushed and breathy. "God, that was more fun than the time I got pushed out of a helicopter. Did Teddy behave himself?"

Adam shrugged.

"Uh-oh. You look like you went ten rounds with Mr. Kittridge's stinkin' sister. What's wrong?"

"Nothing."

"Nothing?" December picked up her bear and stroked its ears. "Oh. You fought with Tess."

Adam cringed. The stuffed bear made for a good spy, at least with December's unique talent. "Yeah, I fought with Tess. But you don't need to worry about it."

"I'm not worried."

He watched her chew her lip and stare at the ceiling for a moment. "What?"

"I said I'm not worried."

"Yeah, I know. I meant to ask what you meant by that."

"She'll forgive you."

"Ah," he leaned forward and tapped the table for emphasis. "It's not my sin she needs to forgive, December. She wronged *me*."

"But," she hugged her bear a little tighter, "you're scared she won't forgive you for...why are you messed up over this?"

Why was he messed up? A deep, bony ache permeated his ass and radiated through his spine. He was mad, sure, and deservedly so, but it wasn't just Tess. Hell, everybody's nerves were frayed beyond recognition. "I think we're cursed. I think Hagatha cursed us all. My family's falling apart December. Grandpa Lum was the one cog that kept it all running smoothly. With him gone, Hagatha's at our throats, my parents, my aunt and uncles, they're all riding this emotional roller coaster without a safety net. And that doesn't even begin to describe what going on between the younger cousins. The twins are acting like they might become upstanding citizens, Sissy's drinking again, Petal's ready to toss the Hippocratic Oath out the window, and Tess. She's been angry for over twenty-four hours now and she's behaving irrationally in public. And when I try to help get things under control, she tells me not to start. Like I'm a thorn in her side or something."

December nodded. "I get it."

After silence drifted through like the transient doctor, he shifted in his seat to get the blood in his backside moving again. "Thanks. For listening."

"That's why my ears are so big, Little Red Riding Hood."

He chuckled. "Well, c'mon Granny. Let's go see what's on the menu."

"Please. I'm so hungry I could eat a bear. Oh, shit, Teddy heard that."

"I think he'll forgive you."

CHAPTER TWENTY-ONE

Wednesday, 3:30 p.m.

DESPITE THE UNIFORM GRAY COLOR OF THE FOOD, Adam enjoyed the stroganoff. He didn't care that the meat was a bit tough to chew or that the noodles seemed made of rubber. It was comfort food, pure and simple.

The company wasn't bad either.

All things considered, it was the perfect first date.

December winked and blushed whenever he looked at her, which made his heart bounce. They played footsie beneath the table like teenagers out of a '60s sitcom. All that was missing was a root beer float with two straws and Jan and Dean singing *Little Old Lady From Pasadena* through a jukebox.

"How'd you end up with that lab coat?" Adam asked as he pushed his plate aside and noticed, finally, that her clothing was different.

"I stole it."

"Clearly." He waved his hand in forward circles. "Care to elaborate?"

A sly sort of smile graced her lips. "So, you saw I took his handcuffs, right? The cuffs sang like a canary, and showed me all the hiding places that guard went to avoid doing his rounds. I found a stash of smokes and diet pills, too, but I didn't take them. So anyway, I ducked into a broom closet until he ran by and then went up to his hiding place on the roof. I traded his handcuffs for his girlfriend's lab-coat and I walked right by him when I came back down. He didn't even notice."

"You're a lucky skunk. I'd've been tackled and thrown in the slammer."

She squished her nose. "It's only 'cause you're the tall one. You kinda stand out."

"I suppose I do." He popped tension loose from his neck and shifted in his seat again. His butt was numb.

"So, do you want to know what the handcuffs said Tess was arguing about, or are you still too mad to care?"

He sighed. "No, I care. I've always cared. It's my curse."

"Okay," she leaned forward, her eyes bright and her words saturated with excitement. "So Tess walks in looking for Mr. Kittridge's stinkin' sister and she marches up to the desk where the security guard is."

"To get a room number?"

"Yeah, but she's also here to see if Spider is here too."

Adam paused. "You mean Chance."

"Duh." Sarcasm. Her eyes darkened. "Who's telling the story?"

He squeezed his eyes shut and forced down laughter. "You're telling the story."

"So the guard happens to be in the middle of reading that *Fifty Shades Trilogy* right? But he's wrapped *The Catcher in the Rye* dustjacket around it so no one can tell. And when Tess asks for the rooms, the guard ignores her."

"Oh, so not cool," Adam winced. Tess never handled poor customer service well. "No wonder things got out of hand."

"Wait, it gets better. He says, 'Let me *ax* you a question,' after completely disregarding her whole inquiry."

"Ouch. That's her biggest pet-peeve. I'm surprised she didn't request his manager on the spot."

"Oh I did," Tess interrupted them. Tell-tale pinks streaked her face, showing the aftermath of tears. She took up the plastic chair at the end and spoke in not-so-Tess-like quiet tones. "I told him I refused to speak with inbred idiots who didn't know how to speak English."

"And that went over like a fart in church, didn't it?" Adam shook his head. "Tess, I'm so sorry. I wanted to diffuse a situation..."

"No, I'm sorry Adam. You're right. The last twenty-four hours, I've treated you and the twins like my own personal doormats, and I really don't have an excuse." She wrung a napkin tight between her fingers, her eyes cast down and away. "I mean, I could plead cramps or hormones, or even that I lost my sanity temporarily, but that would be lying."

Adam nodded, "Yeah, you never had your sanity."

Tess slugged him without malice. "God, what's wrong with us, Adam? What's wrong with our family that we fall to pieces the moment we face a little adversity?"

December snorted. "I hardly think the word little describes anything about Mr. Kittridge's stinkin' sister."

A tear slipped free from Tess's eye, "It hurts Adam. Really hurts. Grandpa Lum, he treated me just the same as the rest of you, and at the wake...I felt like Mike and them all looked at me as an outsider. Someone who didn't belong there."

"Jesus, Tess, is that what this is all about? You think we care that you're adopted?" Adam pushed his seat so he could pull her against his chest in the most supportive hug he could manage.

"Not you or the twins or your folks. Or even Wackadoo, here." Her voice was muffled. "But the extended family, the ones who maybe didn't get as much from the will as they may have wanted."

She was sobbing. Tess wasn't a crier, and yet Adam felt her tears leach through his t-shirt. He squeezed a little tighter. "Well, fuck them Tess."

It was a role reversal that didn't go unnoticed. Tess pulled away, wiping her cheeks. "What?"

"Fuck them," he repeated. "They weren't there every summer, all summer long. They weren't around to laugh at Grandpa's jokes or to help with the farm or anything. Sure they'd all visit once in a while, the occasional Christmas or whatever, but the fact of the matter is: he's *our* grandfather, not theirs. To them, he's a fourth cousin twice removed or some such nonsense. And Grandpa may have had a few things set aside, but we know he wasn't a rich man. He measured his wealth through us, Tess. Through his love for me, and the twins, and our parents and yours, and you. Especially you."

"Why especially me?" Tess hiccupped.

"Are you kidding me?" Adam swallowed the lump in his throat. "The rest of us Grandpa was stuck with. But when Dahlia and Curtis chose you, Grandpa chose you too."

"I will never say this again," Tess said, wiping her nose on the napkin, "and if you tell anyone I said this, I'll deny it. Adam, you are the most insanely perfect person ever in this world."

December tapped her shoulder. "I'm a witness, Tess."

"Shit," Tess turned around and heaved a melodramatic sigh. "I guess that means I'll have to kill you."

There was a long pause. "That's cool," December said. "Can we kill Mr. Kittridge's stinkin' sister first?"

"Good God, I nearly forgot." Tess fumbled through her messenger bag and withdrew a syringe. "I swiped this from the emergency room. I was thinking we could introduce an air bubble into Hagatha's I/V bag. No one would ever know."

CHAPTER TWENTY-TWO

Wednesday, 4:00 p.m.

T ESS REFUSED TO DITCH THE SYRINGE, and she refused to relinquish her murdering rights. Adam decided he'd stick to her like glue. If anyone came to arrest her, they'd have to arrest both of them.

Upon arrival outside Hagatha's room, however, Adam realized there would be little chance for their killing endeavor for a while. Todd stood nearby, flirting with the duty nurse while Adam's parents occupied the room's visitor chairs perusing a garden magazine. Adam exchanged an unspoken conversation with Tess, deciding that family witnesses were undesirable.

December indicated her disappointment with a blown raspberry.

"I'm not supposed to allow so many visitors in this ward." The nurse sighed, a bitter frown developing under sharp, accusing eyes.

Todd flashed his Harrison Ford grin, "Don't give them the excuse to leave. They will. And I need them here so I don't strangle the woman."

"May Heaven forgive me but it's not Ms. Kittridge's welfare that I'm concerned with here." She pulled a pen from behind her ears and scribbled something on her clipboard. "The woman bit me when we admitted her. I had to get a rabies shot, and hepatitis and HIV test so, to be honest, I could care less if you strangle her. But, I do have other patients, Todd. And they have a right not to have your entire family thundering through the ward."

Todd raised his eyebrows. "My entire family? Honey, they're just the tip of the Kittridge iceberg."

From the desk, the nurse lifted a glass containing a pair of dentures resting in a bubbly sludge. "And these..." She shoved the glass into Todd's hand, "I've half a mind to send these home with you, so that if and when she ever comes to, we can't locate them to return them."

A liquid thud resounded from Hagatha's room. Adam heard his father curse. "Uh, I'm sorry," Adam's father poked his head into the hall. "I, uh, knocked over the pitcher of water in here. Is there something we can clean it up with?"

The nurse sighed. "All right, everybody, out."

Adam's parents stepped out, both looking like guilty kids called to the principal's office. The attending Kittridges gathered at the nurses' station as the nurse waved them over. Adam hung his head, disappointed. They were going to lose their access to a convenient murder in three, two, one...

"This is a good opportunity for me to run some tests on Ms. Kittridge. I wish I could say that they are all painful and embarrassing, but she's not going to notice in her coma. I'm still going to ask that you all leave. You can come back in about an hour and a half." The nurse pointed towards the elevators. "I'd appreciate it most if you'd stagger your return so it at least looks like I'm trying to enforce the rules."

"Fair enough," Todd said. He returned the faux-teeth cocktail to the desk. "But I'm leaving these here."

Adam's father offered to clean up his spill, but the nurse refused him. "I'm calling Janitorial now. Shoo."

Adam filed out with his family. "Now what?" Tess whispered.

"Dunno," Adam replied, casting a look back towards the nurse, the immutable barricade. "Perhaps we'll get lucky."

"That doesn't seem to work for us," December said as the elevator announced its arrival.

"Well, I can hope."

"Are we going back to the lobby?" December looked worried.

Todd held the carriage doors open. "Yes. Why, do you have a better plan?"

"Well, no, but there's a certain security guard..."

Tess turned green. "I'd almost forgot about him."

Adam's mother folded her arms. "Tessie Glynne?"

"Grr, I hate it when you get all motherly on me." Tess spun in the carriage and slid into a back corner. "Even my parents can't make me feel as guilty as you can."

"Spill it."

It was a short trip back to the lobby. December kept quiet about inanimate objects telling stories, so the tale Adam's mother heard was missing a few details. It was tale enough, however, so when the doors dinged open, Eileen charged through the lobby and straight to the security desk.

She yanked the book from the security guard's hands. The dustjacket fell to the floor, revealing the real book underneath. Spinning around, she addressed the crowd in the lobby. "How many of you here were ignored by this man reading this book?"

At first, there was no response.

"C'mon, how many?"

Tess raised her hand first, but within a few seconds, at least half the visitors in the lobby had their hands raised also.

Adam's mother turned back around and slammed the book on the counter. "You threaten my niece and you have the nerve to sit there, smug, like no one can touch you?"

The security guard trembled in his hot seat.

Adam's mother continued. "The man behind me is this state's best lawyer ever and he's my brother. Do you know what that means?"

Yes! Go get him, Mom! Adam bit a knuckle to keep from laughing while the guard did nothing.

"It means I don't need deep pockets to go after you, personally, with whatever legal grounds I can. Can you say something similar?"

"No he can't," December hugged her bear with open triumph.

"So, I only see one option for you," Adam's mother drummed the desk with her fingers. "I smell a resignation on the horizon. That is, unless you can come up with a solution I haven't thought of yet."

The security guard stood, an unsteady move even using the desk as a counterbalance. "I apologize, Miss, for ignoring you..."

Eileen tsked. "I seem to recall there were more raised hands in this room than just one."

The guard coughed and started anew. "I humbly seek forgiveness from each poisson here that I didn't show respek to."

"The word is pronounced Respect." Tess was smug.

"Respekd to."

"Close enough," Eileen said, pulling Tess away from the desk. "Unless someone else has a grievance to voice."

Todd clapped his hands and applause erupted from the crowd. Adam's father took Eileen's arm. "That's my girl," he whispered.

Normalcy returned to the hospital lobby in a strong, steady rhythm.

"Mrs. Bingham," Officer Trencher made his approach. Adam felt December's bear on his back as December hid behind him.

Todd stepped forward. "Hey, Danny. Whatchya got?"

Trencher held up a thick manila file. "Um, well, enough, I think. I'm glad you're here too, Todd. I've talked to the coroner and the district attorney. We're going to place Agatha Kittridge under arrest for first-degree murder and a few counts of attempted murder. You're the closest person she has to an attorney, so..."

"Well, I'll be damned all to Hell." Tess folded her arms and shot Adam an unvoiced question with a severe look.

She didn't have to ask. Adam had the same question. Should they try to kill Hagatha anyway?

CHAPTER TWENTY-THREE

Wednesday, 5:00 p.m.

TRENCHER DIDN'T SEEM TO CARE that the nurse might pitch a fit about him harassing her patients. He led everyone back into the elevator armed with his manila file and his badge.

The all-too-familiar odors of sweat, bleach, and must permeated the carriage, the sort of scent that didn't exist anywhere else. Adam wondered how many more times he would have to ride the hospital elevator. He made a hundred or so up-and-down trips during Grandpa Lum's incarceration, and since Hagatha refused to die like a decent human being, Adam figured several hundred trips more threatened his future. But the smell, that would linger in his sinuses forever.

He hated hospitals, if nothing else than for the elevators.

The doors opened to an active code blue. A dozen medics moved about each other at dizzying speeds. December displayed the scene to her bear, and spoke with a tiny voice, "Look, Teddy. A roller derby."

Tess jumped out of the way as a nurse rushed by. "No, this is more like Sacramento airport traffic."

141

A janitor slipped into the elevator carriage behind the Kittridge clan as if oblivious to the chaos. Adam, feeling pangs of sympathy for some stranger's family, envied the janitor's ability to ignore it all.

"Todd!" the nurse from earlier ran towards him. "Todd, it's Ms. Kittridge."

Trencher stepped between them. "Ms. Kittridge, you say?"

"Yes, Officer. Todd, folks, I don't know what happened. The machines she's hooked up to aren't the newest on the block, but they have been recently serviced..."

Todd held a hand up, "Wait, what are you saying here?"

Adam couldn't tell if the nurse was biting her lower lip out of concern or to keep from laughing. "Ms. Kittridge has flat-lined," she said. "It's been five minutes already."

As if on cue, a doctor emerged from Hagatha's room, removing his mask and gloves. His look bore the darkness of medical stress and bedside concern. Hope sparked in the depths of Adam's weary soul. *Please, Dear God, let it be finally over.*

"Mr. Kittridge?" the doctor asked of their group.

Todd stepped forward. "Yes?"

"I'm Dr. Lambert. I've had to call it." The doctor rested a hand on Todd's shoulder. "I'm sorry for your loss."

"You're shitting us," Tess accused him as only Tess could.

Dr. Lambert shook his head. "I'm sorry, ma'am."

"Well, shit," Trencher said. "I was looking forward to arresting her."

Adam's mother, tears shining in the florescent light, flashed a tight smile, "Thank you, Doctor, for your help. Can we spend a moment with her?"

"Take all the time you need."

Adam followed his family into Hagatha's room. This time, there was no doubt she was gone. Her dull eyes were half-open, showing the window to her missing soul. The devil had collected her, but at what cost? Adam thought of a contract, signed in blood, coming back to haunt them all like the premise to a poorly designed comic book.

Adam's mother placed a hand on Hagatha's brow. "What happens now, Todd? Agatha wasn't the sort of woman to prepare for her demise."

Todd sighed, nodding. "I can handle probate. It'll take a while though. It's pretty safe to assume that even if she had made a will, she wasn't in a sound enough mind to do so."

December took the safety-pin off of her bear's butt and stuck the sharp point into Hagatha's toe. Getting no reaction from the corpse, she tossed the safety-pin in the trash. "Like none of you would've done it." she returned the looks she received from everyone.

Adam's mother shrugged. "Well, I suppose you're right."

"Why did you pitch the safety-pin?" Adam whispered in December's ear.

The question earned him a sharp look. "Ew! After I stuck it in her *toe?*"

"Ask a stupid question," Adam winced.

Trencher stepped through the doorway, causing December to duck behind the life-support machines. "The doctors said there was nothing wrong with her," he scratched his head. "A woman that obese and they claim she was healthy as an ox."

"Oh, sure, healthy as an ox. But just a nasty case of psychotic grandeur." Todd smirked.

"She won't fit in a standard-sized coffin," Eileen said. "We'll have to have her cremated."

December poked her head out from her hiding place. "Uh, Mr. Todd, Adam, uh, can I talk to you?"

"Now?"

"Yes, Mr. Todd. Please?"

Adam and Todd joined December in the hallway. "What should I do if I know something about someone's death that's a little hinky, but not so hinky that it's like murder or anything?"

"Was that even English?" Adam asked.

"What do you know, December?" Todd brought a hand to his chin and peered at her over the edge of his nose.

December clutched her bear, stroking its furry ears. "Mr. Kittridge's stinkin' sister didn't die of natural causes...mostly."

"What do you mean...mostly?"

"Well, Mr. Todd, I mean Mr. Kittridge's stinkin' sister died naturally, but she had help."

"What helped her?" Todd asked. "It's okay, you can tell me."

"When Mr. Bingham spilled the water in her room, Janitorial was called right? That janitor, the one we passed at the elevator? He brought in the floor polisher."

"Okay, I'll bite. What then?"

"He unplugged the life-support machine to plug in the floor polisher." December bit her lower lip, pouting. "I feel bad. I know Tess was really looking forward to killing her."

Adam lost his ability to form recognizable speech and could only stammer out a series of grunts.

Todd shook his head, "No, Adam, we can't not tell anyone. What if the janitor has done this to other people?"

Adam, puzzled, wasn't sure that's what he said. He tried again. "No, I mean, let me start over. How do we tell anyone here that cares? Who would we talk to?"

"Oh, is that what you mumbled? I was taking a wild guess," Todd laughed. "I'll get Danny and we'll go have a talk with the hospital director. Don't you worry. But, uh, maybe not tell Eileen. She's been through enough, yeah?"

December handed Teddy to Adam as Todd turned away. "Here, hold him. I've gotta ditch this coat. I'm having some serious flash-backs."

"Uh, sure," Adam said as she stripped off the white lab coat.

"You wouldn't believe the things this girl is into." December whispered behind her hand, "There's a club and they all dress up like mascots from amusement parks."

Adam closed his eyes in attempt to shut out the mental images sneaking into the corners of his mind. Next thing he knew, a small hand gripped the back of his neck and pulled him down, and he landed on a pair of soft lips. His eyes shot open for a moment, just to be sure it was December, before he kissed her back.

From across the hall, he heard Tess groan. "Oh, God, you two. Get a room."

CHAPTER TWENTY-FOUR

Monday, 10:15 a.m.

A DAM WAS LATE. He checked his watch for the third time and sighed, relieved. Fate put him back on track and in familiar territory. He walked up the driveway in time to see a tow truck hook up the boat of a Cadillac. Hagatha's car gave up the ghost when she had, refusing to start for anyone.

December even tried hot-wiring it, unsuccessfully. The twins wanted to douse it in gasoline and set a match to it. Tess talked them out of it, but just barely.

Adam's mother signed some paperwork and handed the clipboard back to the tow driver. She looked tired. It had been one helluva week.

"Hi, Mom," he hugged her. "I'm sorry I'm late."

"You're early," she winked at him when she withdrew. "I really didn't need you here until eleven."

He cringed. He hoped she hadn't just jinxed him.

"Adam, I'm kidding," she poked his ribs. "But it's okay you're late. I doubt anyone will come anyway."

"I know Todd'll be here, eventually." Adam followed his mother up the drive and the path to the porch. "And December'll be here as soon as she scores a good deal on a sow."

She shook her head, opening the screen door to the old Victorian. "Pigs again."

Adam shrugged. "It's fitting."

"Speaking of animals, I haven't seen hide nor hair of Sauerkraut."

His eyes made the slow adjustment to the dark interior of the living room. His heart was heavy. Truth be told, he missed the cat. "Ah, she'll turn up someday when you least expect her, missing another patch of fur and drooling in the catnip."

The living room, like the rest of the house, was papered in colorful sticky notes. It was December's idea. She convinced Todd to let her stay there for the week so she could listen to the furniture in the house. It turned out to be an efficient system. Pink stood for the Archers, blue for Todd, and yellow for the Binghams. Green was reserved for everybody else. In addition to color, the papers each had a name written in black marking pen across their surfaces.

It was like a ticker-tape bomb had exploded in the house, leaving rainbow shrapnel over everything.

"I'm just so impressed with December," his mother said as she moved through to the kitchen. The rainbow shrapnel was prolific there as well. "I never knew she paid this much attention to my Dad's stories. Do you know, she was able to tell me the history behind that mantle clock?"

Knowing the truth, Adam smirked. "She's got an air-tight memory bank, that's for certain."

"I had my doubts about her Adam, and about you two dating. Her family has a history of mental illness and speaking as a mother, I don't want you mixed up with that. Relationships are hard enough without extra baggage. But, I mean, someone who cares this much about someone...I want that for you. It'd be nice if you two could work through it." She filled a mug with coffee and handed it to Adam.

When Adam filed the restraining order against his last girlfriend, his mother crossed her arms and looked at him with her I told you so eyes. Her stance on crazy was always an emphatic *Hell No.* "Mom? Have you already been in the scotch?"

Her hand slammed down on the counter. "Jesus, Mary and Joseph, I have one, ONE, Irish coffee this morning and you're accusing me of being drunk?"

He held up his hands, surrendering. "God, no, Mom. I was...just wondering why...you're not sharing is all."

"Don't lie to me. It isn't healthy."

"Seriously though, Mom, I have no idea what to do when you give me an approval for someone I'm dating." He found the whiskey bottle and poured a splash into his mug. "It's never happened before."

"Hrmph. I liked that one girl, Rosa," she said as she poured another mug of coffee.

He offered her the whiskey but she brushed him off. "You only liked that Rosa was Catholic. You forget she had this thing about chewing her food with her mouth open."

She paused. "Oh, yeah."

Adam spied the casserole dish, still unclaimed on the sideboard. "It's nuts, right? I mean Aunt Agatha knew there was arsenic in her well water, so she bought all those water bottles to drink from."

"Yeah," his mother looked away, as if she could see through the kitchen walls and beyond the neighbor's bull pasture into a forgotten world. "I wonder how much of her deluded mind was caused by her arsenic exposure, although I don't know how it poisoned her if she wasn't drinking it."

"Showers, Mom. The poison probably absorbed into her skin over a period of time."

"That makes sense. And if she washed all her dishes using that water, I guess she was still consuming it." She returned from that world to her coffee. "I'd like to think that maybe she wasn't really that horrible. That it was always the arsenic."

"I'd lean that way too, if it weren't for the fact that she's been horrible since you were a kid. She'd've been dead long ago if that were the case."

"You're probably right. Still..."

Tess announced her arrival through the screen door. "Y'all home?"

"In the kitchen!" Adam's mother called out.

Adam heard the screen door squeak on its hinges and flack shut. "Oh God on acid, why does it look like that Rainbow Sprite threw up in the living room?"

"Mornin' Tess." Adam said as she popped her head through the kitchen archway.

Her eyes widened. "And the vomit's in here, and the dining room, too?"

"The vomit is everywhere," Adam's mother said. "December was very thorough."

Adam sipped his coffee. The alcohol fumes tickled his nose, but warmed the path to his stomach. "I wasn't expecting you here today."

"What, miss the chance to bitch about that miserable wretch of a hag to the family that knew and hated her? Not a chance."

"Are your parents coming?" Adam's mother asked, handing Tess a coffee mug.

"Thank you, Eily," Tess winced through the first sip. "Ow, that's hot. Uh, no, my folks aren't coming. They'll be there to help with the ashes though."

"Well, it'll be a small turnout then. Not many people liked her."

"Mom, let's be honest now. You're the only one who liked her."

"No, I loved her. Like and Love are different animals you know. I never approved of how she behaved. I just respected her as an elder."

Tess looked guilty. "I guess someone had to. I wasn't very good at it."

Adam chewed on his thoughts. He wished he could've respected her too, but there were some people in this world that were beyond redemption. Hagatha was one of them.

Still, he was here. To help his mother sure, but he was still here. And Hagatha thought the world of Eileen. Couldn't that be enough?

December came in through the kitchen door. "I got another pair of Hereford sows, they'll be delivered next week."

Tess frowned, "A pair? We can't name them both Hagatha, or can we?"

Adam's mother shook her head. "We're not naming either one after Aunt Agatha."

"But–"

"No, Tessie Glynne. That's final."

"Oh all right. Pig and Poke, like always then."

Grandpa Lum told Adam once that grudges only serve to poison the soul. Adam would eventually forgive Agatha Kittridge, for the woman she had become. But he didn't have to do it today.

Today, they would wake Agatha in proper Kittridge style and tell stories of surviving the tuna casserole and the fireplace poker. And later, there would be more talk of bats in the barn and pigs in the pen, and of pot-bears and bed-and-breakfasts, and of love and loss and lunacy; those invisible ties that bind a family together.

FINIS

Adam Bingham and December Ashby will return

Also by
Shelton Keys Dunning:

PUBLISHED THROUGH OLDEWOLFF PRINTS:

The Trouble with Henry

PUBLISHED THROUGH BANNERWING BOOKS:

Short Stories / Flash Fiction

Escape (Precipice 2012 volume 1)
Sticky's Cake (Precipice 2012 volume 1)
The Soldier's Gambit (Precipice 2013 volume 2)

Thank You

There are many authors out there and so many good books to read. I am humbled and grateful that *Hagatha Kittridge Must Die* has found a place on your bookshelf.

Sincerely,

S.K. Dunning

P.S. – I invite you to stop by and say hi. The more the merrier!
www.sheltonkeysdunning.com
@SheltonKDunning +SheltonKeysDunning
http://skdunning.tumblr.com
http://sheltonkeysdunning.blogspot.com
http://www.flickr.com/photos/skdunning/

The Cold Side of Trouble

Book Two of the Sy-Frei Adventures,
Sequel to The Trouble with Henry.

Simone Freitag reunites with FBI agent Brian Kirby for another adventure. A body is discovered in a cabin fire just as three teens go missing from a Revolutionary War Reenactment near Brian's hometown of Simplicity Forge. Brian returns to his Smokey Mountain roots when he learns one of those missing teens is his youngest sister, Lucy. But missing teens and murderers have more to fear than the Redcoats and the troubles of an isolated town. A cold–front is coming, and Lucy's kidnapper better pray that Mother Nature finds him before Brian Kirby does.

ABOUT THE AUTHOR

Shelton Keys Dunning has been passionate about reading and writing since she knew words existed, loving the escape from reality that both afford. In her spare time, she knits poorly, takes out-of-focus pictures, runs from spiders, and grows weeds in the dirt. Her husband laughs at and with her every chance he gets. Together they live with a tortoise-shell cat named Whiskey, and dream impossible dreams.